Toys of Desperation

Toys of Desperation

Ben Fry

et alia press

Little Rock, Arkansas

2017

Published in the United States of America by
Et Alia Press
1819 Shadow Lane
Little Rock, AR 72207
Etaliapress.com

ISBN: 978-1-944528-03-4

Cover design by Vladan Djordjevic
Layout design by Eric Pervukhin
Back cover photo by Lonnie Timmons III
Edited by George H. Jensen

The very place puts toys of desperation,
Without more motive, into every brain
That looks so many fathoms to the sea
And hears it roar beneath.

—*Hamlet,* Quarto 2, Act 1, Scene 4

Chapter 1

You can blame it all on Richard Nixon, if you want, although it seems like Richard Nixon gets blamed for a lot of things. All I know is if Nixon hadn't been president and hadn't wanted to be re-elected, and if all those crazy guys that worked for him hadn't come up with that lame-brained idea about breaking into the Democratic National Headquarters at the Watergate complex in order to make sure he got re-elected, and if those so-called "plumbers" hadn't gotten themselves arrested and if those newspaper guys Woodward and Bernstein hadn't kept digging and digging until they found out the connection between the "plumbers" and the President, and if the Senate hadn't decided to call for hearings into the whole Watergate thing, and if Sam Ervin, who was the Senator in charge of those hearings, hadn't decided to get them started in May of 1973 and if those hearings hadn't been televised everyday and interrupted the game shows I liked watching during summer break (not to mention my Mama's soap operas), I would have sat at home on my fat butt and watched TV most of that summer. Instead, my Mama said, "Why don't you go ride your bike?" So I did.

My best friend had moved away just a couple of months earlier. His name was Jim, and he lived right across the street from me. Well, not exactly across the street. More like catty-cornered. You know what I mean. He lived on one corner of the intersection, and I lived on the other corner. Anyway, we had been friends since Miss Mary's Pre-School and had spent every summer together, making up crazy games and playing pretend. Only we didn't call it pretend. We called it "play like." Let's play like we're a couple of big game hunters and we're searching for the lost treasure of the elephant graveyard. Or let's play like we're superheroes, and you've got the power to fly and I've got invisibility and you're my sidekick. Stuff like that. Jim could "play like" a lot better than most kids so we spent most of our time playing together and ignoring the other kids in the neighborhood. Then his stupid dad got a job in another town and they had to move away and I was stuck with nothing to do but watch television and then Nixon and all that came along so I had to ride my bike around.

My bike was okay, but it was no 10-speed. All the bigger kids were getting 10-speeds back then, and I still had a regular bike with a big banana seat. I could pedal it pretty fast, but those 10-speeds looked so cool, and I kept asking my mom if I could get one and she kept saying, "Some day," which usually meant no, but sometimes really meant "some day." I liked riding my bike, even though it wasn't a cool 10-speed, especially in the summer when I wore shorts. I hated riding my bike with long pants because I always seemed to get my pants stuck in the chain. We wore bell-bottom pants in those days, and bell-bottoms were really cool, but they flopped around a lot and ended up stuck in your bicycle chain. Some kids wore rubber bands around their legs when they rode their bikes, but I always thought that looked goofy, although it also looks pretty goofy to get your pants leg stuck in the bike chain, and it was hell to try to get the thing out because you'd have to stop your bike and get off of it carefully and turn it upside down and roll the pedals backwards until you got your pants unstuck and then you'd end up with a greasy hole in your bell-bottoms and that looked pretty goofy, too.

When I rode my bike, I didn't just ride it around the block or down to the railroad tracks and back. I rode the thing all over town. People weren't afraid of letting their kids go all over town back then the way they are now. Now people are afraid their kids are going to get snatched by pedophiles or kidnappers and stolen away for good, but back then in a small town like Weir, Arkansas, parents didn't think twice about those kind of things, even though there was this retarded kid (he really wasn't a kid—he was like 30 years old but he thought like a kid and acted like a kid)that lived in our neighborhood with a bad reputation. One guy I knew said he had called him into a dark alley and tried to talk him into dropping his drawers, but I don't know whether I believe this kid or not. Y'know, kids will say a lot of things for attention, and old Martin, that was the retarded guy's name, really didn't seem like the sort to do something creepy like that. Regardless, I stayed away from Martin, like most of the kids in the neighborhood, which is too bad, because if the story wasn't true, then Martin lost out on making a lot of friends. Mama always told me to stay away from Martin. I don't know whether she'd heard the story or not. She never said. She may have just not wanted to me to play with a 30-year-old retarded guy.

I decided to ride my bike across Billings Street, that was the main street in town and the busiest, and over near the high school. I had just finished elementary school, 5th grade, and was heading on to junior high the next year, but I wouldn't dare ride to the junior high school. It was on the other side of the tracks, and when I say that I mean it literally. The city of Weir had two sets of railroad tracks crossing through it, one going east-west and the other going north-south. At the place where the two tracks intersected was where the city had grown from. There was an old train depot right there that nobody ever seemed to use anymore and downtown Weir had grown along the northwestern corner of the intersection. The tracks that ran east-west separated the business district from the neighborhood I lived in. The north-south tracks separated my neighborhood from where the black people lived. In Weir, in 1973, all the black people lived on the West Side of the north-south tracks and all the white people lived on the east side. I'd been right up to those railroad tracks. I'd stood on them. But I'd never crossed to the other side. Never even rode in a car to the other side of them. But next year I'd be going to school over there.

The schools in Weir didn't integrate until 1970. Most people think the schools in Arkansas all integrated in 1957 because of the crisis at Central High School in Little Rock, but the truth is that most Arkansas schools didn't integrate until nearly thirteen years later. The black people in Weir had their own elementary school and high school across the tracks, and the white people had their own schools on my side of the tracks. The city had enough money to build two new schools for the elementary kids when the schools integrated but not enough for the junior high or high school kids. So when Weir integrated its schools in 1970, all the kids, black and white, went to high school in the white neighborhood, and all the kids, black and white, went to junior high at the former black high school in the black neighborhood. A lot of white people threatened to send their kids off to a private school in another town rather than send them to school across the tracks. But not many white folks could afford a private school and the ones that could afford it were high-minded enough to think it was a good thing to send the kids to school together across the tracks. It was never any choice in my home. Mama and I barely had enough money to pay the rent, much less send me off to some private school, so I was headed to school across the tracks next year, even though I'm pretty sure it made my mama real nervous.

The high school was on my side of the tracks and across that busy Billings Street. The farther east you went in Weir, the nicer the houses and the better-off the people who lived there, for the most part. There were pockets of poor folks everywhere in Weir. Probably even the folks we thought of as rich weren't that rich. But they lived in the farthest eastern edge of town in a place called Saratoga Hills. Saratoga Hills really was hilly. It was part of Crowley's Ridge, a strange little line of hills that run parallel to the Mississippi River in the delta of eastern Arkansas. Below the ridge is a fault line called New Madrid where a terrible earthquake occurred more than a hundred years ago, when there wasn't much more than Indians living in this part of the state. Legend goes that the Mississippi ran backwards during that earthquake, which seems a little far-fetched to me, but a lot of strange things seem to happen in the past that don't seem to happen anymore, so maybe it did. Crowley's Ridge is all filled with this hard, white soil called loess, which isn't found anywhere else in this part of the country. Some folks believe that Crowley's Ridge was once the spot where the Mississippi flowed, and that in prehistoric times when the river shifted, it left a big gash in the ground that got filled up with loessal soil blowing in from Oklahoma. Makes as much sense as anything, especially when you look and see how flat the land is to both the east and west of Crowley's Ridge, as if this little place didn't belong there at all.

I got across Billings without much trouble. They'd put a traffic light in there to accommodate students crossing the road to get to the high school, so you could push a little button and get the right of way. It was a lot easier than dodging traffic. It was also a lot easier than crossing the street in front of Miss McCreary. She was a half-blind, old, retired nurse who drove a great big old jalopy around town. Miss McCreary really hadn't been able to see good for years, so when she came up to an intersection, rather than looking both ways to see if any traffic was coming, she just honked her horn and kept going. Anybody who knew her knew to get out of her way. Thankfully, she avoided Billings Street, where she probably would have gotten sideswiped. But she drove around my neighborhood, usually on her way to the drugstore downtown, and one time I was riding my bike, minding my own business, when I heard that horn honk. I was in the middle of an intersection, and here came Miss McCreary, barreling down at me at a startling 25 miles per hours. I pedaled as fast as I could and just barely managed to get out of her way. I'm pretty sure that if she'd run me over, that the police would have told my mother it was my own dumb fault for getting in the way of the old lady. Everybody knew to get out of Miss McCreary's way.

Across Billings Street, I kept pedaling toward Saratoga Hills. I had a friend who lived up there named Dewey. I'd been to his house a couple of times, and we had a lot of fun together in school. His daddy was a lawyer or something, and they had a big nice house. He wasn't as good at "play like" as Jim, but maybe we could find something to do if he was at home.

As I pedaled down Maple Street, I came to the house of a kid who always kind of gave me the creeps. Her name was Mabel Ann, and the kids all made fun of her because she'd say weird things. For instance, like one time in second grade, we were playing on the playground, and we saw Mabel Ann by herself, poking at something with a stick. There's not a boy alive, then or now, who wouldn't stop what he was doing to take a look at something being poked at with a stick, so me and my friends all went over to check it out. "What you poking at?" we asked Mabel Ann, and she looked at us real serious and said, "It's the devil's claw." The word "devil" always gave you a bit of a start, and when I looked down at it, I have to admit, it looked kind of like a devil's claw. It was dark black and round, with five small digits, each with a sharp talon sticking out of it. She pushed hard against it with the stick, and it seemed to be as hard as a rock.

"That ain't no devil's claw," my friend Marty declared. "It's the paw of an old dog. Probably got killed and this is all that's left of it."

Mabel Ann looked him straight in the eye. "How do you know?" she said, as serious as the grave. "You ever seen a devil's claw before?"

I was a little shaken. I'd never seen a devil's claw and couldn't argue with her logic, but Marty could. "No. Have you?" Then Mabel Ann looked mad. She took the stick and pushed the devil's claw, or dog's paw, or whatever it was, over in amongst all of us boys. All of us, including Marty, took off lickety-split, half laughing, half scared to death. As we run off, Marty said to me, "She's as crazy as a loony bird." I looked back at her, and I'll be darned if she didn't pick up that nasty thing and wave it at us like some kind of evil charm.

Then there was the time in the fourth grade when we were all sitting in our seats reading, or supposed to be reading, while the teacher was grading tests, when the girl all of sudden let out a wild whoop and said, "Get back! Get back! Get away!" We all turned and looked at her, and she was swiping the air like a bee or something was flying around her head, only nobody saw any bees or flies or mosquitoes or anything flying around her. From her chair, the teacher shouted, "Mabel Ann! What's wrong with you?" But all Mabel Ann would say was "Get away from me! Go away!" The teacher got out of her chair and walked up to Mabel Ann. She looked like she was about to scold Mabel Ann when one of the girl's hands swung toward the teacher and smacked her in the gut. The teacher doubled for just a second, then grabbed Mabel Ann by the wrist and marched her out of the classroom and down to the principal's office. No one heard or saw Mabel Ann for a week after that and when she finally did come back to class, she was as quiet as a church mouse. Never said a word nor made any sort of weird noises. If she wasn't working on her classwork or reading, she just stared into space with an empty look on her face, making us all wonder what was going on inside her head.

Mabel Ann lived near the high school, and to my shock, she was sitting in the front yard of her house, playing with a puppy dog and looking as normal as anybody. I guess I was staring at her because she waved at me with a half a smile, and even though I didn't want to, I waved back. My mama had always told me to be polite to people, even if you didn't like them. It wasn't that I didn't like Mabel Ann. She was just so scary.

I pedaled on past the high school to Saratoga Hills. When I started pedaling through those hills, I realized again how much I'd like to have one of those 10-speeds. I'd never ridden one, but I'd heard how you could climb hills with ease if you just geared down (or was it geared up), and pedaling up those hills was kind of hard. You had to stand up and pedal as hard as you could. Even if you were pushing on the pedals as hard as you could, you still just barely moved up those hills. I was glad when I finally got to Dewey's house. I was so worn out I pushed my bike up his driveway and tossed it aside, not even bothering to put down the kickstand. Dewey came to the door and invited me inside while he finished his breakfast. His mom seemed kind of perturbed at me for showing up before he'd finished eating. Of course, it was nigh on to 9 o'clock by the time I got there and most people had finished breakfast by then, but Dewey liked to sleep late during the summer, and I expect that his mama did, too. Dewey was eating cinnamon toast, and his mama reluctantly offered to fix me some, too, but I told her I had already had breakfast, which I had. My mama had made my regular breakfast: four pieces of buttered toast and a cup of coffee. Mama had gotten me started drinking coffee with her when I was just nine, and I liked it. Not so much because I liked the taste of coffee, but because coffee was kind of like beer—a grown-up drink, and it made me feel grown-up to drink it, even if the coffee I drank was half coffee and half milk, with plenty of sugar. Mama didn't like spending a lot of time percolating coffee for just me and her so we drank instant coffee. Just add some hot water. It wasn't until I was a grown man that I discovered how terrible tasting that stuff was compared to fresh-brewed coffee. Live and learn.

I sat and watched Dewey finish his cinnamon toast and watched his Mama watch the Watergate hearings on the little TV in their kitchen area. This was another sign of Dewey's family's prosperity. Hardly anyone had more than one television in those days, and he had a big console TV in the living room and a little TV in the kitchen area. I felt like I'd stepped into some other dimension when I walked into Dewey's house. When Dewey finished his breakfast, he told his mom we were going bike riding, and she said okay, just come back for lunch, and she looked at me kind of funny, like she wondered if I would invite myself over for lunch, too, and I thought I'm going home for lunch because I bet whatever my mom came up with would be better than what she came up with anyway.

Dewey pulled his bike out of the garage, and I was glad to see he hadn't gotten a 10-speed yet either. He said his dad had promised to get him one for Christmas, and I lied and said I was getting one for Christmas, too, even though I had no idea whether I'd get one or not. It just made me feel better to think I wasn't that far behind Dewey. We rode down Dewey's driveway, and that was great because it was steep and we could coast for a long ways down the street before we had to start pedaling again. Dewey said there was a house that burned down over in the Macon neighborhood and that we ought to go take a look at it, and I agreed that it sounded like a good idea.

The Macon neighborhood was near Saratoga Hills but was one of those pockets of poor people on the eastern edge of town. Don't ask me how those things work because I don't know how neighborhoods grow and some rich people will be living in a place and some poor people will be living in an almost identical place right next to it. I think neighborhoods are just concocted by real estate people and don't really rise up naturally at all, except for old neighborhoods like where I lived, which had grown up naturally over several decades.

Macon was hilly, too, so we were having fun riding down the hills, but working hard to get up them. We rode past a row of several small, tightly packed homes when I started to smell charred wood. Dewey slowed down and we rolled up to the burned-down house, a small place, maybe two bedrooms and a little front porch, but it was hard to tell what it looked like because the walls had all burned to the ground. One of the trees outside had burned, too, charred and black with the leaves all burned off of the branches that remained. The houses around it had mostly survived, which told me that the firemen had done a good job at containing the fire. The siding on one house right next door had melted, but none of that house had burned at all. Only the heat had gotten to it. Dewey thought we ought to take a closer look, so we parked our bikes in the front yard and walked up to the front of the house. Not only could you smell charred wood, but you could also smell that putrid odor of burned garbage. Like spoiled milk and rotten bananas. I'd smelled it before when Mr. Reynolds took me to the city landfill. Mr. Reynolds was our landlord, an old man who lived in Little Rock, but used to spend his summers working on the houses and apartments in our neighborhood that he owned, renovating them or building new ones. He worked mostly alone, but I'd befriended him and so he used to let me help him with his work. He used to haul stuff off to the city dump sometimes and that smell of rotting garbage is not one you easily forget.

Dewey wanted to crawl up into the burned mess, but I was hesitant. It looked dangerous, like what remained of the floor could just crash down to the ground at any minute. And I didn't want to get my hands all dirty either. I'd always had a thing about getting my hands dirty. It didn't really get in the way of my having fun—I could make mud pies and play in sand piles as much as anybody, but when I was done, I rushed into the house and cleaned up my hands as quickly as possible. Looking at all this sooty wood and thinking how far it was back to my house and a sink where I could clean up made me hesitant to enter into this big terrible pile of trash.

I was watching Dewey crawl into the burned-up house when something really strange happened to me, something today I even have a hard time explaining. I had this feeling, this kind of outside my body feeling. I couldn't smell anything or hear anything or even see anything for a few seconds. All I had was this sensation, as if I wasn't really there in front of the burned up house anymore, as if I had been transported far away. I felt like I was in the bottom of a well, rock walls all around me, and the only way out was a hundred feet above my head. Then for some reason, the only thing I could think of was my dad. Not the pleasant memories I usually had of him from when I was just a little boy, but scary thoughts. Like something bad was going to happen, and there was nothing I could do about it. I almost cried out for him, but my tongue was just as frozen as the rest of my senses were. I must have looked like a zombie or something because the next thing I remembered was Dewey shaking me and asking if I was okay. The trance, or whatever it was, was over and I looked down to see Dewey's sooty hands tugging at my shirt, and I got a little mad that he had gotten me dirty.

Dewey thought that I must have gotten scared that he was going to hurt himself inside the burned-up house, but I told him no, that wasn't it, but I couldn't tell him about the feeling that my dad was there. Like all my friends, Dewey knew my dad had been dead since I was four years old, and if I told him that it seemed like my dad had been right there with me for a few seconds, he would have thought I was crazy or something. Heck, I thought I was crazy.

I told Dewey that I had to go home, that my mom needed me. He nodded his head and agreed that I should probably go home, but he didn't believe my excuse at all. He thought I'd gone yellow or something and that I was going to run crying home to my mama. Normally, that would have really bugged me, to think one of my friends thought I was scared, that I couldn't handle something. Not that I didn't get scared of things. I was scared of a lot of stuff. I just didn't like my friends knowing that I was scared. This was different though. This was really scary to me. Not just the "I'm afraid I'm going to hurt myself" kind of scared, but the "I don't know what just happened to me" scared that most people never experience.

I pedaled on out of the Macon neighborhood and back toward the high school, leaving Dewey to explore the burned-up house himself. I was a little jealous because I knew there was something about that house that made it special to me, but I was just too nervous to check it out for myself. Maybe Dewey would find something that would help it make sense to me. I'd go see him tomorrow and see what he could tell me.

I pedaled down Maple Street and found the hairs on the back of my neck standing at attention. I turned and looked behind me, only to see that I had just passed Mabel Ann's house. She was still in the front yard, only she was standing. The puppy dog was yapping at her, as she stood there, staring at me, with that vacant look on her face that she used when something was going on in her head, but she didn't want anybody to know what it was. I wanted to turn around and ride back to her and ask her what she was thinking, but I was too scared. I was afraid of what she might say. That it might make sense. That I was becoming a freak show like Mabel Ann. I kept riding, faster and faster. As fast as I rode when Miss McCreary came barreling down on me in her old jalopy. When I finally got back to our old rental house on Jefferson Street, I was puffing and sweating like a convict that had escaped from a chain gang. Mama heard the screen door slam and asked me if I was okay. "Yeah," I yelled back and ran straight for my room. I slammed the door shut and fell onto the bed. My mind raced around like a mouse being chased by a cat. What the hell happened out there?

Chapter 2

I remember the day my daddy died like it was yesterday. At least I think I do. I was only four years old, so it's possible that what I remember are just things that people told me, things I've heard so many times that I just believe them to be my own experiences, rather than the images I've been given from other people's memories. Most kids don't remember things from before they were five years old, but I remember lots of things. I remember looking through a screen door in the back of the farmhouse where I grew up and watching my mama chop up a snake with a garden hoe. I remember watching my daddy march into a rice field and following behind him and my mama calling my name and looking around to see that I was what seemed like miles from the farmhouse and my daddy nowhere in sight. I remember my daddy, a giant, the tallest man in the world, with a flat top haircut and overalls and skin tanned dark brown from working in the fields. And I remember the day he died. At least, I think I do.

It was a Saturday. This I remember because we were sitting on the sofa watching wrestling. We watched wrestling every Saturday morning on a channel out of Memphis. We had an old black-and-white TV with bunny ears, and somehow, fifty miles from Memphis, we got a good enough signal to watch wrestling and everything else that came out of Memphis television in those days. I was sitting on the back of the sofa, up high, so I wouldn't look like such a little squirt, which is what I was. My older sister was sitting on the sofa, and I can't imagine what in the world she was doing there because she never seemed like the sort of person that would like wrestling. Maybe she was shelling peas or doing homework or reading a book or something while the TV was on. Our farmhouse wasn't very big, so there wasn't many other places to go. Two small bedrooms, the living room, and the kitchen, so if you wanted to sit down and work on something, you could do it on the sofa in the living room or at the table in the kitchen, but that was about it. So I guess she was just sitting there with me while I watched wrestling. Not that I liked wrestling that much, but I liked watching anything on television, and the Saturday morning cartoons were over by then, so all I had that was worth watching was wrestling, so there I was.

Mama was in the kitchen, cooking, I guess. She seemed to spend a lot of time preparing meals in those days. I guess it was a lot harder to cook a meal when we lived out on the farm. Not so much prepared foods. Everything was from scratch. My dad was outside. I don't know what he was doing either, but he was a farmer, and he spent a lot of his time outside, even during winter months, studying and planning. He came in the front door and went straight to the kitchen. He and Mama exchanged words, words I don't remember. They weren't bitter words, but they had an air of seriousness to them. I heard the screen door in the back of the house slam, and then heard it slam again, and I decided to investigate for myself. When I came to the screen door in the kitchen I saw my mama and daddy in the back yard, several feet from the door. Daddy faced away from her toward the barren fields and Mama stood behind him with her hand on his back. Their words were again impossible for me to understand, so I went back to the TV where people spoke in loud, clear tones that anybody could hear.

A few minutes later, I heard the screen door slam again, and Daddy came through the living room to the bedroom and closed the door. A few minutes after that, Mama passed through the living room to the bedroom. Then, the next thing I remember is seeing Mama and my older sister standing over the bed, Daddy stretched out on the bed face down, and the two of them looking and sounding afraid. I came and looked at my daddy, whose eyes were shut and whose body was motionless. They both seemed concerned that he wasn't moving, but I assured them he was playing possum, and that he was awfully good at it. Later, Mama told me that his skin turned black then blue. That I don't remember at all. All I remember is this giant of a man, my father, stretched out on that bed. It was the last I would ever see of him.

My only memories after that are sketchy. I remember being at the hospital, in a waiting room, with my mother and my sister, both of whom were crying, and my trying to assure them everything would be okay, even though I had no idea what happened. I remember a lot of people at our house, but I don't remember the funeral at all because no one took me to the funeral. I guess they thought it would be too much for a four year old to see his father put in a box and buried in the ground. I made my mother cry months later when we drove past the hospital and I told everyone that that is where my daddy lived now.

My dad was dead, dead for a long time. I'd seen him die myself, even though I didn't know it at the time. He was kept alive, in a way, by the stories my family told about him and the respect and love that was still given him, even after he had passed on. But there was no doubt that he was dead and gone. No doubt for me at all until that day I had felt his presence at that burned up building in the Macon neighborhood on the east side of Weir, Arkansas, in late May, while the television blathered on about Watergate, and Dewey Barnes teased me about being afraid of my own shadow.

It wasn't my shadow I was afraid of.

The next day, my mama wanted to go to town to buy a few things, and she asked me to go with her. It was only about five blocks to downtown Weir from where we lived, a short walk, which was good because my mama didn't drive. She had driven once in her life, when she was a young mother, some 30 years before. She was married to her first husband then, the father of my older sisters. He was a terrible drunk and would stay away from home days at a time. He had promised to drive my mother and her sister and all their children to town for a picture show. Saturday came and there was no sight of him. It was the 1940s in rural Arkansas and lots of people didn't drive back then, especially women. But my mother was so mad she decided to drive the kids to the movies anyway. She had paid close enough attention to her husband's driving to know how to start it and get it going. With her sister at her side, and the kids all in the back of the pickup truck, she took off for town. It wasn't until she got to a sharp turn in the road that she realized she didn't know how to slow the thing down or stop. "Whoa!" she yelled and pulled back on the steering wheel like the reins of a mule wagon, but the truck kept going, off the road and into the ditch. No one was hurt seriously, except for my mother's ego, and she never sat behind the wheel of an automobile again.

We had to cross the east-west train tracks to get into downtown Weir, where we could go to the five-and-dime and over to the mom-and-pop grocery store my mother liked. They had built a couple of bigger grocery stores out on Billings Street, but they were too far to walk to, and Mama didn't like them anyway. Even though she wasn't much of a talker, she liked dealing with the old couple that ran the mom-and-pop store. They liked to talk more than Mama did, but she felt she could trust them.

Both sets of train tracks that ran through Weir were built up on levees so that you had to climb a little hill to cross the tracks. One time, Mama fell down one of those hills as she walked across the east-west tracks back home. She had fallen on some glass and cut her knee up really bad. She didn't need stitches, but then again, she didn't go to the doctor either. Like most old country folk, she tended to herself as much as she could. She had doctored herself with merthiolate and rubbing alcohol and eventually got better. But she always had a fear of climbing those little hills after that. She had fallen on the north side of the road, the side that was closest to our house. After that, there was never a time that we didn't cross over to the other side of the road before we got ready to climb the hill and cross the tracks. She never said anything, but it must have seemed to Mama that the north side of the road where she had fallen maintained some residue of her accident, some bad blood, or voodoo, or something that made that place scary and forbidding to her. Places sometimes seem that way. Years later, I visited Dealey Plaza in Dallas where President Kennedy was shot, and I had this creepy feeling like

I'd walked into some evil place I shouldn't be. Hundreds of cars still drive through Dealey Plaza everyday, and dozens of people walked down that sidewalk on the north side of the railroad tracks in Weir, but that doesn't make that eerie feeling go away. It certainly didn't for my mother.

After we crossed the tracks and walked among the two-story brick buildings that lined the streets of downtown Weir, I asked my mother a question that had puzzled me since the day before. I hadn't really wanted to ask her because I was afraid she would ask me why I wanted to know, and I really didn't want to tell her why. But I decided I could be evasive without lying to her. I could never lie to my mother. She would know it quicker than anything. But I could just keep my mouth shut. Something she had taught me how to do herself.

"Mama, did Daddy ever live in the Macon neighborhood?"

"Macon? No. Your daddy never lived anywhere except out in the country. Except for when he was a young man and he traveled up north to work in a button factory. Except for then he never lived anywhere except on the farm his daddy built. Not that I know of, anyway. Why do you ask?"

"No reason," I said, and she left it at that.

The next day when my mama looked at me sitting in front of the television watching some Senator grill a guy in a dark suit about what the President knew and when he knew it, she told me again, "Why don't you go ride your bike?" So I did.

Only I didn't ride to the east. I rode west to the railroad tracks and rode my bike on the tracks, trying to see if I could spot the junior high school without actually crossing over to the other side of town. I must have ridden a mile or so north, down the tracks, looking over to the west side, my teeth chattering every time I ran over a railroad tie. The amazing thing to me was that the houses on the west side of the tracks didn't seem much different than the houses on the east side. The closer you lived to the railroad tracks usually the poorer you were. After all, who would want to live right next to the railroad tracks with trains chugging by all hours of the night blowing their whistles and waking you up? We lived three blocks from the railroad tracks, and the trains were loud enough for us. I could only imagine how people who lived right on the tracks must have felt. So the houses on the north side of the tracks looked kind of beat up and uncared for and so did the houses on the south side of the tracks. I wondered if all the houses on the west side looked like that, or if like on the east side, the farther you got from the tracks, the better the houses looked. I did know that there wasn't nearly as many houses on the west side as there was on the east side, and I was pretty sure there wasn't any equivalent to Saratoga Hills on the west side of the tracks. Nothing but bean fields and rice patties that far west.

I saw three black kids standing on the tracks a few hundred feet ahead of me. They were standing around talking, but when they heard me, they stopped and stared. I put on my brakes and looked at them. I'd been going to school with black kids since the third grade, and I knew a few, and some I even considered to be friends, but I didn't recognize these boys. They might have been a little older than me, maybe seventh or eighth graders. If they'd been white, I probably would have rolled on up to them, said hi, and kept on going. But there was still this tense feeling you got when you saw a black kid you didn't know outside of school, a feeling that you couldn't quite put your finger on. I wasn't really afraid, but I was cautious, as if a black kid was more likely to pick a fight with me than a white kid or a black kid had something against me, even if he didn't even know me, just because I was a white kid. I decided to turn my bike around and head back down the tracks toward home. I looked back once and was glad to see that the black kids had just continued talking to each other, ignoring me and not chasing after me. I wondered if they felt the same way about white kids that I felt about black kids.

The worst trouble I ever got from a kid wasn't a black kid at all, but a big, mean white kid. His name was Travis. In the fourth grade, we shared restrooms with the classroom next door to us. There was a little hallway between the two classrooms, with doors on each end. On one side of the hall was a rack where you could hang your coats and on the other side was a boys room and girls room. One day, I asked permission to go pee during class and walked into the hallway, closing the door behind me. Travis appeared from the other doorway. He was a Special Ed kid. The Special Ed class met in that room next to us while the regular class went to science. Somebody told me Travis was supposed to be in sixth grade, but had failed twice. He was a full head taller than me and his long fingernails looked like they were painted because he never cleaned them. I tried not to look at him as I walked into the boy's restroom, but he shoved his way in after me, closed the door and turned off the light. "If you make a noise, I'll kill you. I've got a switchblade," he threatened. I was scared, but I was too scared to take him seriously. I pushed this boy with his big muscles and his growling voice against the wall and rushed out of the darkened restroom. I returned quickly to my seat and didn't tell anybody what happened because I was afraid Travis really would try to kill me if he heard that I ratted on him. Strangely, I think he respected my bravery because he never bothered me again.

I heard a whistle blowing in the distance, so I rolled off the tracks, onto the east side, of course, and watched the train come barreling down the tracks. It was a freight train. I'd heard of passenger trains in stories and seen them in movies, but I'd never seen anything but a freight train on the tracks rolling through Weir. It was a Missouri Pacific train, with 47 cars, including the engine and the caboose. I counted every one of them. All the boxcars and flatbeds. I saw the engineer and waved for him to blow the whistle for me, which he did and I thought I saw someone in the caboose, but I wasn't sure. I didn't see a single soul riding along in any of the freight cars, even though I knew people stole rides on trains some times. My daddy did during the Depression. When the crops were failing and he could find no jobs in Arkansas, he jumped a train here in Weir and rode all the way up to Illinois. He found a job in a factory that cut mussel shells into buttons and worked there for about a year, sending money back to his family and keeping just enough to stay alive. His brother Arnold had gone with him. When they'd earned enough money, they jumped another train and came back. Arnold went on to war in World War II, while Daddy stayed behind to take care of the family farm. When Arnold returned, he starting jumping trains again, looking for work. Only he missed one time in the railway station in Stuttgart, fell across the railroad tracks and got run over. He was buried in the same country graveyard where my daddy was buried, only he had a military tombstone. The date of his death was 1944. If you didn't know better you'd think he'd given his life for his country, instead of for a free ride on a freight train.

Thinking about my daddy made me want to go back and look at the burned remains of that house in Macon, but I didn't like that queasy feeling it gave me. Instead I thought maybe what I needed was some more information.

I pedaled toward Billings Street to the fire station. There was only one fire station for the city of Weir, right in the middle of town, and right on Billings. I had gotten to know the firemen be-cause they had come to visit our home a couple of times. Mama had a bad habit of catching the kitchen on fire. It seemed to always involve melting grease. When you fry up something in a pan, you get a lot of grease left over, and if you don't do some-thing about that grease right away, it congeals and gets stuck to the pan. You can't wash it out. You wouldn't want to anyway because you don't want to wash that grease down your sink. So the best way to get it out of the pan is to heat it up until it be-comes liquid. Then you can pour it in a used milk carton and toss it away. With as much fried food as we ate, Mama must have melted a lot of grease in her day. So many times that occasionally she would forget she was doing it. One time, she was ironing clothes in the living room, watching her stories, that's what she called her soap operas, and letting the grease melt in the kitchen. She turned around to see smoke pouring from the kitchen. So did she calmly put down the iron and walk out of the house? Of course not. She slung the iron across the room and ran for the telephone, not to call the fire department, but to call my sister on the other side of town. My sister told her to get the hell out of the house and she did, throwing the phone across the room, too.

My sister couldn't call the fire department either because she was still connected to my mother so she had to go to the neighbor's house and call. Fortunately, the fire was contained in the kitchen and the iron didn't seem to cause any trouble in the living room. Mama was sure our landlord, Mr. Reynolds, was going to kick us out of the house, but Mr. Reynolds was a kind man and understood. He understood the second time she caught the kitchen on fire, too, only he understood with a little less grace than he had understood the first time.

One of the firemen was a fat old fellow named Mr. Avery. He had been a fireman almost all his life although he'd spent the first few years picking cotton. He once told me he'd rather run into a burning building than ever spend a day in the hot sun, bent over and picking cotton off of prickly cotton plants. A few seconds of danger far and away made up for a whole day of pain and anguish to him. Mr. Avery was sitting in the front room of the firehouse, reading a hunting magazine when I walked inside.

"Hey, there, young 'un!" he shouted. "Your mama ain't tried to burn down the house again, has she?"

"No, sir. She's been playing it safe here lately," I told him.

"Good! Good! What're you doing here today?"

"I had a question for you." I tried not to sound too mysterious because if he thought I was snooping too much into other people's business, he might just shut down and not tell me anything.

He sat his magazine down on the table and leaned toward me. "Alright. What you got?"

"That house that burned in Macon the other day..."

"Oh my goodness," he shouted. "What a terrible fire! Thank God, there weren't nobody to home. Otherwise, we'd a been calling the coroner for sure. Burned clear to the ground. You seen it?" he asked.

"Yes, I have..."

"We were lucky we got there when we did. Place caught fire in the middle of the night. If we'd been a few minutes later, the houses on both sides would've caught fire, too. Lord, Lord. What a mess! What a terrible mess!"

"Who lived there?"

"Let me see," he said, putting his finger up to his temple as though he could push the thought out of his head and into his mouth. "What was that feller's name? Casserole? Naw, nobody has a name like that. Carasole?"

"Carasell," came a voice from behind Mr. Avery. It was a younger fireman I had seen before but couldn't remember his name. "Like a merry-go-round, only spelled different."

"That's it, by gum," Mr. Avery proclaimed. "Carasell. Justin Carasell. Not from around here. Family was from Memphis, I think."

"Nashville," the young fireman corrected him.

"That's it. Nashville. Music City, U.S.A. Must be exciting living there. Wonder why in the world he'd move to a little town like Weir when he could be living in the country music capital of the world?"

"Maybe he didn't like the big city," the young fireman suggested. "Maybe he'd rather live in a small town, where people knew their neighbor's names and where people minded their own business." The young fireman smiled at me knowingly at this last line.

"Yeah, that's for sure. People in big towns are just yackety-yack about other people's business all the time. Just look at those big city newspapers. Never give a person a chance to breathe. Always publishing stories just ain't nobody's business. Justin Carasell. What a funny name!"

"You know anything else about him?" I asked.

The young fireman had gotten interested. He pulled up a chair and sat down beside Mr. Avery. "Why you want to know? You making an investigation?"

I tried to look as nonchalant as an 11-year-old boy could. "I rode by there the other day on my bike, and I was just wondering about the place."

"You going to ask if the fire was intentional or not?" he asked.

"Intentional?"

"Yeah, you know, arson."

"You mean somebody burned the place down on purpose?"

"Is that right?" Mr. Avery interjected. "I hadn't heard that."

"That's because nobody's for sure yet. They had to call in a fire investigator from the state police to look at it. Something kind of suspicious about the way the fire started. In the backyard. State Fire Marshall came by to look at it a couple of days ago. Says he'll have a full report by the end of the month. Now, why is it you wanted to know?"

I couldn't help but feel a little under suspicion, the way that young fireman looked at me. "Just wondering. Saw the place had burned down. Just wondering if anyone had gotten hurt." I started backing away toward the door.

"See you the next time your mama burns down the kitchen," Mr. Avery joked.

"What's your name again?" the young fireman asked.

"Mr. Avery will tell you all about me. We go way back," I told him and flew out the door. I heard Mr. Avery laughing and stuttering around trying to remember my name as I made my way back to my bicycle and back toward home.

Justin Carasell from Nashville, Tennessee. Owned the house in Macon. Place burned down under suspicious circumstances. Mr. Carasell was not there when it burned. And maybe, just maybe, that house had something to do with my dad. That is, if you believe in feelings and premonitions. And honestly, I don't. I don't put much stock in anything like that. Yet for some reason, the whole thing gave me the willies. If Richard Nixon hadn't gotten himself in all that trouble, I'd just be sitting at home watching television, and I would have never known any of this stuff. Just good old fat dumb ignorance at work. Only not this summer. This was the summer when ignorance took a vacation.

Chapter 3

Okay, so maybe the vacation didn't last that long. The television networks, which had all broadcast wall-to-wall coverage in the first days of the Watergate hearings, were losing money like a 5-year-old with hole in his pocket. They could sell advertising in those game shows that I loved and the soap operas my mama loved, but not in the Senate hearings. So guess what? They got together, yeah, the three network execs got together, and decided to rotate the Watergate hearings. One day, CBS would broadcast them. The next day, NBC would broadcast them. The next day, ABC would broadcast them. Then it would rotate around to CBS again. Two days out of three the networks would rake in the dough and on the third day, they would serve the public interest. Of course, a lot of people would argue that game shows and soap operas were in the public interest, too. More interesting anyway than them old white guys fussing at each other.

So I was back to my television addiction. I was glad, too. Being outside, being on my bike, I kept wanting to go back to the Carasell house, wanting to dig a little deeper. At the same time, I wanted the bliss of ignorance, too. And I wanted to watch my game shows!

My favorite was *Split Second* with Tom Kennedy, one of those guys that was always hosting game shows. Three contestants got three related questions and a "split second" to answer each. If you could answer all three questions, you got one amount. If you answered two questions, and one of the other contestants answered a third, you each got less. If each contestant answered one question, you got even less. The winner at the end would pick a set of keys and match it up with one of five cars to see if he would drive off with the grand prize. I mostly loved the questions. My friend Jim and I made up our own version, using a trivia book I'd gotten for Christmas.

I took a couple of weeks immersing myself in *Split Second* with its three questions and *Match Game* with its risqué fill-in-the-blanks and *Concentration* with its giant rebus, and I was happily ignorant. So yeah, I couldn't watch any of them for three days in a row. But it was kind of like I was a contestant on *Split Second*. If I couldn't get all three, at least I could get two.

Then my mom decided I needed some exercise.

Mama's sister, my Aunt Velma, lived on the north end of town, on the other side of the downtown businesses. Aunt Velma was kind of a mess. Even though she wasn't much of a drinker herself, she was addicted to alcoholics. Mama's first husband was an alcoholic, but she learned her lesson and married my dad, who only drank occasionally. Aunt Velma just kept getting involved with alcoholics again and again, to the tune of three bad marriages. She even shot one of her husbands. Actually, she didn't shoot him. She shot at him and missed, but the cops were called and it was kind of a stink for a while. She had several kids, too, all grown now. None of whom visited her much, except to ask for money, which of course, she didn't have much of to start with. She worked as a maid, cleaning up people's houses. She'd had several jobs over the years, working at restaurants and grocery stores. For some reason, she liked cleaning up people's houses best. I think she liked to nose around other people's business, and cleaning up their houses was a perfect excuse to look in all their closets and drawers and see what they were hiding from the rest of the world. Mama loved Aunt Velma anyway and always felt sorry for her. So she was always thinking, what can I do for Velma?

Mr. Reynolds, our landlord, came by with a couple of sacks of pecans. Some friend of his or his son's friend or somebody had picked a whole bunch of pecans and given them to him. He appreciated the gift but couldn't stand pecans. "I only like 'em if they're baked in a pie, and I don't like pie that much," he told us. So we had two sacks of pecans, which seemed fine to me, because I love pecans. I love to crack them, and I love to eat them, but Mama said it was a lot more pecans than two people had any right to, so she said we should take a sack to Aunt Velma, which meant that I should take a sack to Aunt Velma, since Mama couldn't drive and I had my bicycle.

I was going to suggest that Mama just call Aunt Velma and tell her about the pecans so she could come get them herself. She had an old Buick, after all, that seemed to get her around town just fine. But I figured Mama would view that as disrespectful. My mama almost never yelled at me, except when I talked back. "Don't dispute me!" she'd say. If I heard that, I knew I had crossed the line.

Mama did not consider that riding a bike with a sack of pecans was not that easy. This wasn't any sort of cloth bag with a string I could tie to the bike. It was just a paper sack. I tried to balance it between my legs and on the handlebars, but the pecans made it slip all over the place. Finally, I just kind of snuggled the sack under my arm and held the handlebars with one hand. At first, I found myself riding all over the road because my balance was off. I was heavier on one side and pulling too much on the other. After three or four blocks, I got it worked out and had pretty good control of the bike. I was just glad that Miss McCreary was nowhere in sight.

It seemed like an especially long ride to Aunt Velma's house. Balancing the pecans and keeping the bike moving straight was hard enough, but driving through downtown Weir meant I had to maneuver around a lot more cars. Okay, okay, this is no New York City we're talking about here, but for the most part, I didn't have to deal with more than one car at a time passing me when I drove around a neighborhood. Riding through downtown, I found myself riding right along with a line of cars, having to stop at traffic lights, and watch out for pedestrians, too. Harrowing. I was glad when I got to the other side of downtown and back into a row of houses.

Aunt Velma lived in a small house she rented from a man who lived in a bigger house next door. The man had built the little house several years ago for his mother-in-law to live in. When his wife's father died, his wife insisted that his mother-in-law move in with them. He would have none of this because his mother-in-law drove him up the wall, always berating him and telling him that he wasn't good enough for her daughter. His wife, however, kept after him until he came home one day with a pile of lumber and some concrete and built a little one-bedroom house on the corner of his property. That way, the mother-in-law could live with them, but not "with" them. The mother-in-law had died several years ago, and the wife had divorced him, and he had re-married, but he continued to rent the little house out to people like my Aunt Velma, who were all alone and needed a cheap little place to stay. As part of her rent, she cleaned up the man's house, and no doubt found a lot of interesting things in his closets.

Aunt Velma invited me inside when I got there. Mama had called so she was expecting me. She gave me a hug and thanked me for riding the pecans all the way there. Then she insisted that I sit down and have a glass of ice tea with her. She told me about how the Kensingtons were fighting and would probably get a divorce and how Johnny Rayburn ("You know Johnny Rayburn, don't you?") had fallen in with a bad crowd and gotten himself arrested up in Searcy. She had a whole laundry list of gossip to share with me despite the fact that I could care less. Then a thought occurred to me.

"Do you know anything about Justin Carasell?" I asked.

She put her finger to her lips and thought. "Justin Carasell? Hmmmm." Somewhere in the file in the back of her head, the name popped up. "Oh, you mean the fellow whose house burned down a couple of weeks ago?"

"Yeah."

"Not really. He was from out of town. I don't know why he was living here. I don't think he had a job here in town or anything. Kind of a loner from everything I've heard. Why you want to know?"

"Ah, just saw the house after it burned down. Heard the name and wondered if you knew anything about him."

"No. Can't really say. I can ask around though."

"That's alright. Do you know anything about the house?"

"The house?"

"Yeah. Like who else lived there before him."

She stared into the sky and her brain began processing years of gossip and tall tales.

"No. No, I can't think of who lived there or anything special about the place. Just a house. A little old house that burned down. Y'know, the Arlow's house burned down a few years ago. You ever hear how that got started..." And she was off on another story that I can't remember anything about.

When I escaped Aunt Velma's, I felt free. Not just because I had left her incessant gossiping behind, but also because I no longer had the burden of carrying that blasted sack of pecans. I could ride fast and free, make donuts in the middle of the road, pop wheelies. I decided to spend some time enjoying my bike. I crossed Billings Street.

Billings cut all the way through town, running north-south, parallel to the train tracks that separated the whites from the blacks. If you stayed on Billings, it turned into a highway, which led to Interstate 40, which ran east-west all the way across Arkansas. East would take you to Memphis, Tennessee. West would take you to Little Rock, the capital of Arkansas. I'd been to both Memphis and Little Rock. I'd gone with some friends to Memphis to visit the zoo and go to a movie. I'd been to Little Rock more often. I had an older sister who lived in Little Rock. Mom and I used to go visit her during the summer for a week at a time. Sometimes we'd ride the bus and Jenny would come pick us up at the bus station. Sometimes my other sister Layla and her husband Ron, who lived near us, would drive us halfway to

Little Rock and Jenny would meet us halfway. Sometimes when we would meet, we'd stop at this great barbecue place in De Valls Bluff and have dinner together. Then we'd walk across the street and have dessert at this pie shop. Then sometimes, when everyone was in a hurry, Ron and Layla would meet Jenny just off the Biscoe exit on I-40, where there was nothing but a bean field. That always felt a little creepy, meeting somebody on the side of the road in the middle of nowhere. It felt a little like we were up to no good, as if we were crooks in some cheesy movie making a "drop." And me and Mama were the "drop"!

I don't know whether it was coincidence or my subconscious at work, but I suddenly found myself riding my bike through the Macon neighborhood. I was so close to the Carasell house, I decided to ride by, even though the thought made me a little nervous. As I neared the remains of the house, I noticed that the smell of smoke was gone. Then when I pulled up, I found that not only was the smell gone, so were all the burned timbers. Someone had cleaned the place up in the two weeks since I'd been there. The only thing that remained was a concrete slab. I parked my bike in the front yard and walked onto the slab. This would be a great place to play basketball or four-square. A nice, smooth concrete slab with no obstacles sticking up anywhere. I took out a pretend basketball and began bouncing it around the slab, shooting baskets and hearing the crowd roar when I made a shot. Then I heard something else. Not a crowd but a single voice. A whisper. "Put that down!" the voice said, with force and contempt. "Put that down, now!" I stopped dead in my tracks. Had a neighbor seen me playing and wanted me to go? Had Mr. Carasell come up when I wasn't looking? I made a 360-degree turn around the perimeter of the house, looking for the owner of the voice, but no one was there. No one but me. As I stood there, thinking about the voice, wondering where it came from, I realized I had heard that voice before, a long time ago, when I was barely old enough to remember, but I did remember. It was a voice I'd heard hundreds of times before, but never so angry, never so serious and harsh. It was clear though, and though the voice was just a distant memory, I was certain, I knew who it belonged to. It was my father's voice.

Chapter 4

I rode as fast as I could, all the way back to my home. Now it was more than a feeling. I had proof, physical evidence, that my dad had some relation to that house. That it was more than just my imagination. I had heard the voice as clear as a bell. Not just once, but twice, speaking clearly and precisely. Giving an order. To someone. Someone who wasn't there.

I stopped my bike on the side of Maple Street. A voice? What kind of proof was this? I heard a voice that sounded like my father. There were probably a million explanations for it. "It was the wind." "You were thinking about your dad." "It was probably a TV set in somebody's house." "It was an echo from far away." "You're crazy." The last one seemed like the one most people would pick out. "You're just a crazy little kid with a big imagination who misses his dad." The funny thing is, I didn't really miss my dad. I was so young when he died, I only had sketchy memories of him anyway. I remember sitting on his lap in the easy chair, and I remember he let me sit on his lap one time when he was driving and we steered together through this big curve. I remember how he wore overalls everyday, and how he made sure that I had overalls to wear that looked just like his. I remember how he took me one time to see Santa Claus without telling my mama, and how he surprised her with a picture of me and Old

Saint Nick. And I remember stories my mama told about him, like how he searched all over the county for a toy combine to give me for my birthday. And how one time, they were shopping at the dollar store and the owner got mad and was talking mean to one of the employees and how my dad gave the owner what-for because he didn't think it was right to treat a person that way. And how he and Mama stopped going to the little Baptist church down the road from our farmhouse because the members of the congregation wanted to kick out a young woman who was getting a divorce. Of course, Mama and Daddy had both been divorced, and they knew that there were good reasons to leave behind a spouse.

With all the stories I heard about my daddy, he always seemed alive anyway. Not here with us, but alive, like he was still there in that hospital where we left him. My personal memories of him were so minor that I didn't really miss him the way you miss some-body you've been really close to. He was more real to me in those stories my mother told than in my own memories, so his spirit al-ways seemed to be right there with me. But this voice I heard and this feeling I had were different. They weren't from this spirit-Dad that I had come to know. They were from a flesh-and-bones Dad, one that I remembered faintly, but remembered nonetheless.

I pedaled back home at record speed, faster than I had pedaled home the first day I encountered the Carasell house. When I got home, I threw down my bike and beelined it to my room, with Mama in the kitchen yelling, "Did you get those pecans to Vel-ma?" "Yes, ma'am!" I shouted as I slammed my bedroom door.

When something strange happens to you, it always feels good to go somewhere familiar and safe. My room was that sanctuary. It was safe and private, decorated with posters and furnished with toys and gadgets. One wall was covered with posters of my favorite comic book characters: Spider-Man, the Incredible Hulk, Fantastic Four, the Silver Surfer. One corner had a pile of plastic models I'd put together: cars and battleships and the USS Enterprise from Star Trek. In another corner was my cassette deck and the old portable typewriter my sister had given me. It was all stuff that defined who I was or at least who I thought I was. And I could close the door and shut out the rest of the world. In fact, I had the only bedroom in the house with a real door.

We lived in part of a house that Mr. Reynolds, our landlord, had divided into three apartments. Our apartment consisted of a living room, which led directly into a bedroom where my mother slept, which led directly into the kitchen. Off my mother's bedroom was the only bathroom, and off the living room was my bedroom. Originally, that room had been part of another apartment on the other side of the house, but Mr. Reynolds liked me so much that when one of his renters left, he gave us that room and we bolted off the other end of it. The apartment that was left on the other side became very tiny. "An efficiency apartment," Mr. Reynolds called it. The house also had another "efficiency" apartment in the back.

At the front of the house was a huge screened-in porch, as big as any room in the house. The concrete floor of the porch was lined with cracks that went every which way. Jim and I used to drive our Matchbox and Hot Wheels cars along those cracks as if they were roads. There was a porch swing, too, so Mama would often sit there and watch us play. If you looked at the Reynolds house from the outside, it looked like a haunted house. To us, it was a castle.

That night, Mama made stew. Her recipe for stew was dependent on what was left in the pantry. Corn, green beans, okra, pinto beans. She poured it all in a big pot with some beef and somehow this mishmash became simply heavenly. She always baked some cornbread to go with it, light and fluffy and just perfect with stew. The smells had lured me from my room, and I sat at the kitchen table slurping away at the stew. It wasn't unusual for Mama and me to get out our TV trays and eat dinner in front of the tube. Since it was just the two of us, Mama didn't have any trouble eating in the living room and replacing conversation with television dialogue. It mostly depended on what was on TV. Since supper was ready before the evening news was off, we decided to sit in the kitchen.

I thought about telling Mama about hearing Daddy's voice at the remains of the Carasell house, but I couldn't imagine what her response would be. Instead, I asked her a question, which I posed in as innocent a way as I could.

"Did Daddy ever get in trouble with the law?"

I don't know what possessed me to ask this, other than the seriousness of Daddy's voice when I heard him say, "Put that down. Put that down, now!" His voice had an intensity that reminded me of characters in a cop show, like Mannix or Steve McGarrett. Only I knew my dad had never been a cop.

"Trouble with the law? Your daddy? No. Not from the time I knew him. He wasn't perfect, by any means, but he always walked the straight and narrow."

"What about hopping trains?" I asked.

"A man don't hop trains to break the law. Not in those days. A man hopped trains to feed his family. If it's against the law to take care of your family, then I guess your daddy was guilty."

I nodded my head and broke off a piece of cornbread to dip in my stew. I barely got the cornbread wet before Mama took a deep sigh and shook her finger.

"There was one thing," she proclaimed. "He wasn't really breaking the law, but he could have gotten in trouble for it."

I put the cornbread down and moved forward, turning all my attention to Mama. "What was it?"

"You probably remember, we used to hire colored boys during harvest time?" I did remember but I cringed a little at the word "colored." I knew Mama didn't mean anything bad by it. That's just the way she referred to black people. Even at the age of 11, I knew that word wasn't right, that it was hurtful. At least Mama didn't use that other word.

"We had a colored boy working for us one time who got in some kind of trouble. Papa never said what it was, but he liked this boy and apparently he thought it wasn't fair, whatever the law had out for him. Papa already knew that the Sheriff was looking for the boy, so when he come to the farm, Papa told him about the Sheriff, gave him some money and told him where he could go to get away. If the Sheriff had known Papa did that, he would have been madder than a wet hen. Probably would have hauled him into jail himself. Didn't matter to your daddy. Papa always thought that you follow the law, as long as the law is fair. But if the law ain't fair, it ain't the law no more."

"Did the fellow get away?"

"I think so. Don't rightly recollect. Papa and I never talked about it after that."

"What do you think he did? The black fellow, I mean."

"Wouldn't take much. Colored folks were always getting in trouble with the law back then. Guess they still do. Don't really know any colored folk anymore so I don't know what it's like for them. All I know is, your daddy used to say that if white folk got treated the same as colored folk do in this country, there'd be a revolution."

If you looked at a picture of my father, with his overalls and his greasy hair and his solemn expression, you wouldn't imagine him a civil rights activist. Activist is the wrong word, anyway, because other than this story my mama told me, he didn't seem active in trying to help blacks get better treatment. Nonetheless, by his appearance, he looked just like every other redneck farmer in Arkansas, who thought that black people were troublemakers and ought to stay on their side of the tracks. Yet there was something deep in his soul, maybe that sense of justice, that made him see what was wrong and say something about it.

I went to bed that night feeling really proud of my papa. He seemed even taller than he had the day before.

Still, the story Mama told me didn't answer the question of what the relationship was between Daddy and that house in Macon. I know this may sound dopey to you, why I would believe that the voice I heard was real, why I felt so compelled to find out what it meant, why I wouldn't just let it go and forget about it and try to have some fun. Maybe you've never had anything like that happen to you. Maybe you've never heard something or seen something you couldn't explain. Maybe you've never been anywhere that made your skin crawl or made you breathe hard.

Maybe you've been lucky enough to have lived your whole life and never been touched by something invisible and unidentified. If that's true, I don't blame you for thinking I'm a little crazy. Or maybe it's not that you've never had one of these experiences. Maybe you just never wanted to admit it to anyone else.

Daddy had an experience like that, according to Mama. It was before I was born, before he and Mama were married, but after he had divorced his first wife. He was on the farm, the same farm I lived on the first four years of my life. My older brother Curtis was about fifteen, and he and Daddy had gone for a walk after supper. They had stopped to look at the night sky, leaning against an old wooden fence that one of the neighbors had built, when they both saw a flash of light. A bright flash. It glowed for a second and then sank into a field a couple of miles away.

"A falling star!" Curtis told Papa, but Papa said nothing in return. Papa had seen falling stars before, meteorites, and this one looked different. It also landed awful close to home.

It was too dark to check it out that night so they went home and went to bed. The next morning, before they did their chores, the two of them walked into the fields to where they had seen the light drop. They stepped off acre after acre of land, for a while together, and then breaking up and looking individually so they could cover more ground. They searched for more than an hour but never saw any evidence of a meteorite or anything else falling out of the sky. It couldn't be their imagination. They'd both seen it. They'd seen it drop to the ground. Yet there was nothing there.

They never found out what it was, and they never told anyone about it at the time. If anyone else had seen the light, they never said anything either. It was only years later that Papa told it to Mama, and only then if she promised not tell anyone else. I guess after he died, she figured the promise was lifted because she had told me the story on more than one occasion.

Papa and Curtis weren't the only ones in my family with strange stories to tell. My sister Layla had seen a ghost in our apartment one time. It was before she and Ron got married, when she was still living with us. She and Mama slept in the same bedroom, that room that was between the living room and the kitchen. She woke up one night and saw an old woman standing at her bed. She thought it was Mama at first, but then she turned to Mama's bed and saw she was there sleeping soundly. For some reason, Layla didn't scream. I can't imagine why. If I saw someone in the house in the middle of the night that didn't belong there, I'm pretty sure I would have screamed my head off. But Layla didn't. She watched the old lady walk toward the kitchen and disappear. Layla turned over and fell back to sleep. The next day she told Mama, who told her it was just a dream. But Layla contended it wasn't a dream. What she'd seen was real. But she never saw the old lady again and none of the rest of us did either.

I guess that's my point. Sometimes we experience things that just don't make sense. It's easy to dismiss them, say it was our imagination, or a dream. But if it happens to you, it seems too real. Nobody wants to feel like they can't trust themselves.

So I decided the next morning that I wouldn't tell anybody about what happened because they would just make fun of me and try to convince me that it was nothing. Instead I'd try to figure it out for myself, make sense of what I heard my daddy say and why I felt the way I did when I was at that place. I decided, though, that I couldn't do it all by myself. That I needed someone with more experience, who had encountered these kind of weird circumstances personally. I needed an expert.

Chapter 5

Mabel Ann was sitting on her porch, playing with that little dog when I rode up to her house. The dog was a little brown mutt, not more than a couple of weeks old. Mabel Ann had a piece of string that she kept running back and forth in front of the dog, which kept the puppy in constant motion, leaping and running and getting a purchase on it every once in a while, then pulling hard and growling as Mabel Ann pulled back and giggled.

Mabel Ann seemed genuinely shocked when I pulled up into her driveway and across the yard to her front porch. "Hi, Mabel Ann," I greeted her, as if I had stopped by her house a thousand times before. "Is that a new puppy?"

"Yeah," Mabel Ann said suspiciously. "I got it for my birthday."

"Your birthday? When was your birthday?"

"Last week." Mabel Ann tossed the whole piece of string on top of the puppy's head and stepped off the porch toward me. The puppy rolled into a ball and kicked and fought at it.

"What do you want, Billy Williams?"

"Nothing. Just thought I'd say hello."

"We've known each other since Miss Mary's Pre-School, and you ain't never said one word to me."

"I don't think that's true."

"Yes, it is. You're just like every other boy in this town. You talk about me and call me mean names when you think I'm not listening. What you don't know is, I hear a lot more than folks give me credit for."

"I tell you, Mabel Ann. If I've ever said anything to hurt your feelings, I apologize. That just ain't right, and my family'd be ashamed of me if they knew."

Mabel Ann seemed to let her guard down. She sat down on the steps and picked up the puppy, which barked and licked her, making her giggle. In all the years I'd known her, I couldn't recall ever seeing her so happy and carefree. One of those mean names we called her was "Miserable Ann," because she always looked like she was dragging the weight of the world behind her. This was a different side of Mabel Ann.

Taking her light expression as a sign of peace, I hopped off my bike and sat down beside her on the steps. I reached over and scratched the puppy behind the ears.

"What's his name?" I asked.

"Groucho."

"He doesn't look grouchy to me. Looks pretty happy."

"I didn't name him Groucho because he was grouchy, stupid. Look." She picked up the puppy and showed me his face. "See how dark black his eyebrows are. And his black nose looks like a mustache."

"Yeah?"

"Groucho. He looks like Groucho Marx."

I couldn't really see the likeness, but I agreed anyway. Then I tried my best Groucho imitation. "That's the most ridiculous thing I ever heard," I proclaimed, flicking an imaginary cigar in the air. Mabel Ann burst into laughter. Either my imitation was really good or really bad. Either way, it made her laugh.

Mabel Ann didn't look nearly as creepy when she was laughing. In fact, she looked downright normal. Any of my friends who came along at that moment would be shocked to see her like that. They would be even more shocked to see me sitting on the porch, talking to her. Man, would I get some ribbing over that. It's bad enough when an 11-year-old boy is seen in the presence of a girl. But sitting right next to the creepiest girl in school, on her porch, while she laughed her head off, I was just asking for trouble.

The thought of it made me jump up from my seat and step back. Mabel Ann stopped laughing and snuggled her puppy tight to her chest. "What do you want?" she asked, with a look on her face like she smelled something stinky.

"I wanted to see if you wanted to go bike riding."

"Bike riding?"

"Yeah. Grab your bike and let's go for a ride."

"I don't got a bike."

"What?"

"I don't ride bikes."

This was getting far more complicated than I expected. How was I going to get her to the Carasell house if she didn't have a bike to ride? I could suggest we go for a walk, but that sounded even more suspicious. And it was a pretty good walk from Mabel Ann's house to the Macon neighborhood. She'd probably give out on me before we got halfway. I couldn't believe what came out of my mouth next.

"You could just ride on the back of my bike."

If I thought the guys would make fun of me for sitting next to her on her porch, I don't know what they would say if they saw her riding on the back of my bike. I'd end up as ostracized as her.

She stared at me for a long time. I could see her digging into the expression in my face, trying to figure out whether this was some kind of trick, that she was being set up for an embarrassing moment. For my own part, I tried to maintain an inviting smile, although I'm sure it looked shaky and less than sincere. My palms were sweating, and I could feel my neck getting hot. Finally, she put squirmy little Groucho over her shoulder and said with almost no emotion at all. "I'll be right back." Then she turned and walked into the house with the dog.

I wondered if she'd come back out with a pistol or an older brother or a furious dad. She came out a few moments later all alone. She had a bounciness in her step, but her expression still seemed neutral, uncommitted. "Let's go," she proclaimed.

Getting Mabel Ann balanced on the back of my bike was quite a challenge. She had to sit at the back of my banana seat, which meant I had to sit uncomfortably toward the front. There was no place to put her feet so she had to stick them straight out. Worst of all, she had to put her hands on my hips to hold herself steady. I got a cold chill up my spine when she touched me. What in the world was I doing? I was worried that people would make fun of me if I told them what happened to me at the Carasell house. Was this supposed to be better in some way?

We rolled along carefully north toward the Macon neighborhood. Surprisingly, Mabel Ann was easier to carry than a sack of pecans. She didn't slip and slide all over the place. In fact, she kept pretty good balance for someone who didn't ride bikes.

The longer we rode the less her hands felt like knives stabbing into the side of my body. Once when we came to one intersection, I had to put the brakes on fast because of an oncoming car. With the sudden jolt, Mabel Ann's hands wrapped around my waist. Almost as quickly, she slipped her hands back in position on my hips. The really strange thing about this was how nice it felt.

My experience with girls up to this point had been varied and inconsistent. There was the girl, same age as me, who lived across the street. We had started our relationship by throwing rocks at each other. In the second grade, there was this girl who used to follow me around the playground all the time. One day, she dared me to pull up her dress. Never dare an 8-year-old boy. Got in a lot of trouble over that. Then there was Clementine. She sat in front of me in third grade. Her hair smelled like wild strawberries. She lured me behind the teachers' parked cars one day and gave me a big kiss. I was in love. She moved away at the end of the school year.

As we rode toward Macon, I forgot that Mabel Ann was Mabel Ann. I guess I was imagining Clementine hanging on to the back of my bike, her fingers pressed into my side. I even started to hum the song. "Oh, my darling. Oh, my darling. Oh, my darling Clementine. You are lost and gone forever. Dreadful sorry, Clementine."

"What are you humming? Or trying to hum?" Mabel Ann asked indignantly.

"Nothing," I responded. The moment was gone. Lost and gone forever.

"Where are we going anyway?"

"I want to show you something."

We finally arrived at the empty lot where the Carasell house had once stood.

"Is this it?" she asked.

"Yeah."

She got off the bike and looked around. Then she swirled around and looked at me with angry question marks in her eyes.

"There was a house here," I explained as I got off my bike. "It burned down a couple of weeks ago. They've cleared it off since then. Dewey Barnes and I saw it right after it burned."

"Anybody die?" she asked.

"Not that I know of."

She stepped onto the concrete slab and inspected her surroundings. "Somebody died here."

"I don't think so. I talked to the firemen, and they said the place was empty when it burned."

Mabel Ann flopped down in the middle of the slab and sat there, her legs crossed like some kind of swami or Buddha. She closed her eyes and concentrated. I would have thought she looked crazy if I hadn't experienced some bizarre things at this place already.

"It may not have been in the fire," she said, her eyes still closed, "but somebody died here. I can feel it."

I walked over to her and bent down on my knees. "How do you feel something like that?"

She opened her eyes. "You just do. Ain't you never felt something you couldn't explain?"

I did not answer. I didn't want Mabel Ann to know. I sat down next to her, taking a similar position. "Who died?"

"I don't know." She closed her eyes and started to concentrate again. "I think it was a long time ago." I closed my eyes, too, and we sat there, concentrating. I was trying to hear the voice I'd heard before. For some reason, with Mabel Ann sitting there, it didn't seem so scary. But I didn't hear anything. Not a voice. Not even a whimper. Just a dog barking in the distance. Then Mabel Ann mumbled something. It sounded like, "Daddy."

"What did you say?" I asked.

"Nothing. I didn't say nothing."

"I thought you said, 'Daddy.'"

Mabel Ann seemed nervous. "No. It wasn't me."

"Well, then who was it?"

"Maybe it was him." Mabel Ann pointed in front of us.

Dewey Barnes was standing there, straddling his bike. "What are you doing?" he asked in shock.

I leapt to my feet and started dusting myself off. "Nothing. I ain't doing nothing."

"What's SHE doing here?" Dewey asked, pointing at Mabel Ann.

"What are YOU doing here?" Mabel Ann responded, unperturbed by the situation.

"None of your business."

Mabel Ann stood up. "Well, it ain't none of your business what I'm doing here either."

Dewey turned toward me. "Were you sitting with her?"

I stammered. "I wouldn't call it 'sitting with her'..."

"What if he was?" Mabel Ann interrupted. "What difference would it make to you?"

Dewey stepped off his bike and came toward Mabel Ann. "It'd make quite a bit of difference. It'd mean he's as crazy as you and needs to be locked up in an insane asylum."

Mabel Ann moved right into Dewey's face. I hadn't seen her this confrontational since she had that run-in with the fourth-grade teacher. "So you think I need to be locked up in an insane asylum, huh?"

Dewey wouldn't back down. "That's right!"

"I think you ought to be locked up in the county jail for disturbing the peace. We were minding our own business and along you come, sticking your nose in and causing a big rigmarole."

"Oh yeah?" I guess Dewey had run out of clever things to say. "Yeah!"

I realized if I didn't do something, it was going to be a real shoving match between the two of them. I stepped up and grabbed both by the shoulder. "You two cut it out. Somebody's gonna get hurt."

Like a mirror image, they both wriggled out of my grip. Dewey turned toward me.

"Are you sweet on her or something?"

I gently pushed Dewey back so I could talk with him out of Mabel Ann's earshot. "You know I'm not sweet on her."

"Then why are you with her?"

I looked back at Mabel Ann. Her expression had become pouty, perhaps begging me to stand up for her, like I should have. Instead, I concocted a story. Not quite a lie, but not quite the truth either. "I brought her here to look at the place," I whispered, "because I thought she might have some funny things to say about it."

"Funny?"

"Yeah. You know how she's always seeing and hearing things that aren't there. I thought if I brought her to a place like this, she might really have some funny things to say about what happened here."

Dewey contemplated my proposal for a moment, then looked at Mabel Ann. "Yeah. I guess I can see that. Did she say anything funny?"

"She might have if you hadn't interrupted us. Now, I'll never get anything out of her."

"Okay. Okay. I'm leaving." Dewey walked back to his bike. He turned and whispered to me. "Just tell me what she says later." He turned and flipped his middle finger up at Mabel Ann, who returned the gesture by sticking her tongue out at him. He quietly careened down the road and back toward his home at Saratoga Hills.

Mabel Ann walked up to me. "What did you mean, you wanted to hear me say something funny?"

I realized that Mabel Ann really did have super-sensitive hearing. "I was just telling him that to get rid of him."

"So that was it. This was just some kind of trick to get me to come up here so you could make a fool of me. I should have known." Mabel Ann started marching away, back in the direction of her house.

"No, Mabel Ann. That's not it." I grabbed my bike and walked it toward her, rushing so I could catch up with her. "I wasn't going to make fun of you."

"Right!"

"Listen, Mabel Ann. If you'll stop and listen, I'll tell you the truth."

Mabel Ann did stop. She turned and looked at me, her face full of rage. "The truth. What truth?"

I stopped. Suddenly, I felt very nervous and afraid. I had made the decision not to tell anyone about what happened and only one day later I was prepared to tell someone who wasn't even my friend. On the other hand, it would be good to share it with someone, and of all people, Mabel Ann was the least likely to make fun of me over it.

I pushed my bike up against a big oak tree that had grown next to the sidewalk. The tree's giant roots had contorted the concrete walkway until it look like waves of frozen water. I sat down on one of the concrete waves and let all the tension of the past two weeks flow out of my arms and legs. I guess Mabel Ann could see that I was really bothered because she ended her flight. She came and stood over me, looking down.

"Why don't you sit down?"

"Aren't you afraid one of your friends will make fun of you?"

"I don't care."

I motioned for her to sit next to me on the wavy sidewalk beside the tree. She sat down and looked at me, trying to still look cold and angry, but letting a little wisp of sympathy ooze out around her eyes.

I told it all to Mabel Ann. How I had come to the burned-up house and had the weird feeling about my father. What I'd found out from the firemen and my Aunt Velma about the house and the man that lived there. How I'd come back later and found the empty lot and heard a voice I thought was my father's. The stories my mother had told me about my father. And how I'd decided to come get her to go with me to the lot, in hopes that she might help me learn some-thing more.

"So you believe that I have some kind of power to see and hear things that other people don't?"

"I don't know. But I know one thing. While we were sitting there together on the concrete slab, I'm almost sure I heard you say, 'Daddy.'"

"Yeah."

"So did you hear my father's voice?"

"No, I didn't."

"Then why did you say, 'Daddy'?"

Mabel Ann hesitated for a moment and looked off into the distance. "Because I heard my daddy's voice."

Chapter 6

Mabel Ann's father had died in an automobile accident a couple of years earlier. At least, that's what Mabel Ann told me. I didn't know anything about it. Not surprising, since I never talked to Mabel Ann or even paid much attention to her up until then. Maybe it had been announced on the PA system or a teacher had mentioned it when Mabel Ann was out of school. I just didn't remember anything like that. Maybe the teachers didn't care about Mabel Ann anymore than the kids did.

Mabel Ann's father was a truck driver. He was gone a lot of the time, on the road. He drove a big rig, an eighteen-wheeler, from one side of the country to the other. In those days, the government didn't regulate the amount of time that a trucker could spend driving each day, and truck drivers might try to keep driving for 18 hours or longer without sleeping. I had heard that truckers often popped pills to stay awake, but Mabel Ann didn't say anything about that.

Somewhere in Arizona, after her father had been driving for who knows how long, his truck blew a tire. The truck jack-knifed and Mabel Ann's dad lost control. He wasn't wearing a seat belt, so he ended up flying through the windshield and crushing his head on the rocks. He was dead before he ever reached a hospital.

Despite being away from home so much, Mabel Ann and her dad were close. They would go fishing together (something I never imagined Mabel Ann doing), and he would tell her stories about things that happened on the road. Like one time he was eating lunch in a truck stop in Kankakee, Illinois, when this smelly guy with long, dirty hair walked up to him and accused him of being an alien.

"I'm no alien," Mabel Ann's daddy said. "I was born right here in the United States of Kiss My Ass." Mabel Ann said her daddy was always saying things like that, except when her mama was around.

Come to find out, the fellow didn't think her daddy was from somewhere south of the border, but from another planet. It was then that her daddy looked at the guy's eyes. "I tell you, baby girl." That's what he always called Mabel Ann. "I tell you, when you looked deep into that feller's eyes, you could tell he was the one from another planet. His eyes were spinning two different directions at the same time, like pasties on a hootchy-kootchy dancer." Mabel Ann had to explain to me what pasties were and why they would be spinning in two different directions. From her description, I figured out what a hootchy-kootchy dancer was, but I was embarrassed. Not because of the way she described it to me, but because I didn't know what she was talking about.

The crazy guy wouldn't give up on his accusations. He was making the rest of the restaurant nervous, especially the waitress, who was afraid she was going to have to throw the guy out. Finally, Mabel Ann's father gave in. "I admitted, baby girl, that I was in fact from another planet and that I had arrived there in Kankakee in a fine-looking spaceship, built by little green men on the planet Mars. The feller got all quieted down and started talking real softly. I guess he was so used to people telling him he was wrong all the time that he didn't know what to do when somebody agreed with him."

Then Mabel Ann's father invited him out to look at his spaceship.

"The tractor-trailer rig?" I asked.

"That's right. Daddy walked him over to the far side of his truck and asked the fellow what he thought of his spaceship. The guy squinted his eyes up real small and looked at the truck careful- ly. 'That ain't no spaceship,' the crazy fellow admitted. Before he could say another word, Daddy's fist hammered into the fellow's jaw, and he dropped to the ground like a bag of wet cement."

"Your daddy sounds like he was a tough customer."

"Just when you riled him up. He could've just left him there in the parking lot, and let somebody run over him. Instead, he dragged him up to the front of the truck stop and leaned him against the wall. Daddy didn't know whether he was drunk or crazy, but he decided it wasn't up to him to do anything about it, one way or the other. He just wanted to keep him from getting in any worse trouble."

Mabel Ann's eyes gleamed when she talked about her daddy. To her, this was a heroic story, about her father's compassion and wit, rather than the tale of a tough guy who punches out some poor crazy nut. I wasn't going to argue with her. Who was I to judge somebody else's memories?

I asked Mabel Ann what she heard her daddy say at the Car- asell house.

"I'm not absolutely sure," she admitted, "but it sounded like, 'Leave it to me.'"

"Leave it to me?"

"It was kind of soft and mumbled, but that's what it sounded like. At first, I thought he said, 'Leave it to Beaver,' but I couldn't think of any reason Daddy would want me to watch an old TV show. Although, he really liked that show."

I had hoped to get some answers by taking Mabel Ann to the Carasell house. Instead, I got more questions. Why would I hear my father's voice, and she hear her father's voice? Had the two of them known each other in life? Doubtful. My father was about twenty years older than her father and worked on a farm. Her daddy had driven trucks all his adult life and grew up in another part of Arkansas. Was it just that we were both two kids whose fathers had died, and we desperately wanted to hear their voices? I would have thought that Mabel Ann was faking it, but I never said a word to her about what I had heard or felt until after she revealed her own experience. I asked Mabel Ann if she had ever heard her father's voice some other time since he had died.

"Not like this. I've heard his voice in my head, telling stories, like the one I told you. But it's in my head, in my memories. This was something different. This was a voice I heard coming from somewhere else. And it was my dad's voice. And it wasn't any memory."

I thought for a moment about the next thing I was going to ask Mabel Ann. I thought she might get mad and go home, but I wanted to know. "Mabel Ann, kids been making fun of you for years for the strange things you say, and the way you act some-times. Half the kids think you're crazy, and the other half think you have some kind of weird voodoo power. What's the deal?"

She turned and looked right into my eyes, serious but not mad. "Which half are you in?" she asked. "You think I'm crazy or a witch?"

"Let's say right now, I'm not in either group. That's why I'm asking."

She studied on the question for a moment. "It's funny. You say a few things people can't figure out, and you act a little different than everybody else, and people start trying to call you names. Weird. Crazy. Scary. Look at you. How long do you think it would be before your friends started treating you the way they treat me if you told them what you've told me today? Heck, you're even afraid to be seen with me, like something might rub off on you. And what you're afraid will rub off on you isn't my weirdness or craziness or scariness, but the names they call me. You're afraid of being called names. You're afraid of being like me."

I turned and looked across the street. I wanted to deny what she said, but she was right. I was afraid of being treated like an outcast. Like Mabel Ann. The easiest thing to do would be to forget the whole thing, to pretend like it never happened. Never tell anybody. Mabel Ann would know, but I could just deny it. People would believe me, not her. After all, they all thought there was something wrong with her anyway.

But I didn't want to deny it. I didn't want to ignore it. I wanted to understand it. I wanted to know why Mabel Ann and I stood at this place and heard our fathers' voices. I wanted to know if my dad was trying to tell me something. Was it important? Or was it simply connecting with him that was important? And why was Mabel Ann's dad there, too? I wondered if you lined up a group of people and sent them to stand in the place, one at a time, how many of them would hear the voice of a dead relative? Was this a magical place, like a fountain of youth? Was it a time warp? A tear in the universe that you could step through and go back in time and through space, like that big glowing stone circle in that Star Trek episode? Was this a house on the "edge of forever"?

I turned back to Mabel Ann and smiled. "Y'know," I said, "you're really cool."

She blew a raspberry and laughed.

"No, I'm serious. You've been really great to me. Really honest. Thanks."

"You're welcome."

I rode Mabel Ann back to her house. I wasn't nearly as nervous on the way back, and I didn't mind at all that she had to hold on to my hips. I didn't even have to imagine that she was Clementine. I'm not saying I fell in love with her or anything like that. She just didn't seem quite so creepy to me anymore, and I didn't seem to care so much that anybody else thought she was creepy. It was kind of a relief.

Unfortunately, I had not answered any of my questions about my father and why I heard his voice at that place. I had only gotten more questions. Perhaps the answers I was looking for were not to be found at the Carasell house. Perhaps what I really needed to know was more about my father. My mother had told me so much about him, but what I really needed to know were things my mother didn't know. There was only one person I could think of that could fill in those gaps. I hadn't seen him in years, but he was as big in my memory as my father. In some ways, bigger. I called him Mr. Butt.

Chapter 7

His real name was Buttram. Big Don Buttram. But when I was two years old, I declared he was "Don Butt." He was a big man, a couple of inches shorter than my dad, but twice as round. He was big in his manner, too. Loud and funny. His laugh sounded like a cannon blast. He loved my dad. They'd been friends, long before my mama and dad got married. He had known Daddy's first wife, had helped him get through that situation. He had stood by him during the divorce when others wanted to stay away from him. He had accompanied him on the wild goose chase to find me a toy combine when I was a boy. He had probably accompanied him on lots of wild goose chases over the years. He probably knew more about my dad than anybody else and could tell me secrets that maybe Mama didn't even know. But he lived way out in the country, near our old farm, 10-15 miles away. Too far to ride my bike, and besides, I wouldn't even know which of the little houses along that stretch of dirt road was his.

When I got back to the house that afternoon, Mama had pulled out the folding table and set up a jigsaw puzzle. A couple of times a year, Mama would work on a puzzle. She had four or five stored away in a closet somewhere, five-hundred pieces or more. She'd spend an hour or two a day working on them, carefully matching the colors and the shapes. The pictures were always things you wouldn't expect an old lady from the country to care about. This one looked like a painting of Venice, with gondoliers on their boats and medieval buildings stacked along a canal. We'd worked on this one at least two or three times before that I could remember. When I got there, she had already put the edges together. Whenever Mama put away a puzzle she'd finished, she would take all the edge pieces and put them in an envelope and throw that in the box. She didn't see any value in sorting out the edges from the rest of the pieces again. If she could get the edge pieces laid out to start with, she could get right to the guts of the puzzle immediately, which is what she really liked.

She'd placed two cane-backed chairs next to the table, one for her and one for me. I sat down in the one she'd left for me and started sorting through pieces of blue sky and clouds. Jigsaw puzzles were kind of like television, something you could do together without having to come up with a lot of chitchat. That didn't mean we sat there silently. We just didn't need to fill up a lot of empty space.

"You hungry?" Mama asked me. It was well past noon.

"Naw," I lied. "I'll wait."

We picked through pieces for a while, and then I got up my courage to ask a question, as innocently as possible. "How come we never see Don Butt anymore?"

"Don Butt? I saw him the other day."

I craned my head. "You did?"

"Yeah. He trades down at Meyer's, just like us. All the country folk come to Meyer's."

"Where was I?"

"Off riding your bike, I guess."

"Do you think he goes down there often?"

"Once ever week or two, I guess. That's what we used to do when we were in the country." For the first time since I got home, Mama looked up from the puzzle. "What you asking about Don Butt for?"

"Just thinking about old times."

Mama nodded her head and looked back at the puzzle. "Me, too."

Mama kept her emotions to herself for the most part. I'd catch her crying every once in a while, and if I did, she'd quickly dry up and get about her business. I'd ask her what was wrong, and she'd just say, "Nothing." Sometimes I'd find her staring out the window, with a solemn look on her face, her brow twitching with some thought or memory she was trying to work out. I think she missed my father, even though she never said such. You could tell it more by the way her voice would light up when she talked about him.

My father had rescued her, in a way. Mama's first husband was a mean drunk. He'd always been a drinker, but something happened to him in World War II. He came back telling Mama stories about men getting "Dear John" letters on the island where he was stationed in the South Pacific and walking into the propellers of airplanes. These visions twisted him and made him suspicious of my mother, which led him to drink more. And the more he drank, the meaner he got. He would chase Mama and the girls through the house with a butcher knife, threatening to cut them up in little pieces, like an airplane propeller. Then he would disappear for days on end. No word. Not a trace. Sometimes he would show up sober and apologetic, promising to do better, get a job, support his family. Most of the time, he showed up drunk again, and prone to violent outrages. Mama grew tired of it and did something extraordinary. She filed for divorce.

Divorcing your husband in rural Arkansas in the 1950s was just about unheard of. Even if your husband was beating you within an inch of your life, you stayed married. It was God's way. Mama, however, was never a very religious person. The most important thing in her life was her children, and if her drunken, no-good husband threatened them, he had to go. There was much talk about it and a church committee was formed to discuss the matter with her. She wouldn't even let them in the house.

Some people supported her. She always spoke fondly of the sheriff, who stood up in court and testified on her behalf about how many times he'd had to drag her husband off to jail and how he believed the man to be a threat to her and her children. And there was the anonymous folks who left food for them on the front porch when her husband disappeared for several weeks and left the family without a dime.

Mama's divorce was granted, finally, and the no-good drunk abided by the law for some reason and left the family and the county, never to be seen again. Some of his kin heard that he had moved out to California, and Mama always said that she hoped he slipped in the Ocean and floated back to that little South Sea island that had messed up his brain so bad.

Unfortunately, Mama was left with no visible means of support. She and the girls had spent many years squatting, moving from empty shack to empty shack. It was common in those days for people to just move into a vacant home and take it over until they heard about something better, or until someone came along and ran them off. Mama said there were a couple of places they lived in more than once. And while her ex-husband hadn't produced enough money for them to buy or rent a place, he had usually come up with enough cash to get them some food and a few clothes now and then. Now, even that was gone.

Mama heard about a man named Williams, Wynter Williams, who had a sickly mother he needed looking-after. Wynter Williams had also divorced recently. His wife had taken his daughters and moved up north near her folks, leaving him with his teenage son and his invalid mother to care for. Wynter Williams owned his own farm, a homestead that his father had made claim to at the turn of the century. It was everything a turn-of-the-century homestead in eastern Arkansas could be. A rattle-trap old place with a metal roof and a porch big enough for a whole family of dogs to live under. Wynter had made some nice adjustments to it, like that lovely blue-gray asbestos siding to prevent fires from spreading. He hadn't quite gotten around to putting in a septic tank, so the toilet was still settled in the outhouse out back. Still, it was better than the shacks where Mama and her girls had nested for so long.

Wynter Williams hired Mama on the spot to take care of his mother, cook meals for him and his son, and generally keep the inside of the house respectable. In exchange, Mama got some spending money and a place for her and her girls to live. It was a sweet deal except for one thing. Wynter Williams' mother was as mean as a snake with a toothache. She had no kindness for

Mama, always cursing at her and calling her names. Maybe she was just mad that she was so sick or that she'd lost her husband years before or that her son had to hire a woman to come take care of her, instead of his wife. Regardless, Mama persisted and did what was needed to take care of the old lady. Then one morning, Mama went in to clean her up and get her ready for breakfast and found her lying there as solemn and peaceful as the first day of spring. She was dead, of course. It was the happiest Mama had ever seen her.

It was shortly after Wynter's mother had passed that Wynter and my mama got married. Wynter's son was happy (he liked Mama's cooking) and Mama's girls were happy (they liked having a place to live with a daddy who didn't chase them around the house with a butcher knife), but best of all, Mama was happy. Wynter was solid and kind, and he made Mama feel special. Neither one of them had been quite so happy as when they were together. And while they did all they could to prevent it, their happiness spilled over into a child a few years later, born to a woman in her 40s and a man in his 50s. They hadn't planned to have a child together, but then again, they hadn't planned much of their life to turn out the way it did.

It wasn't until after my father died that Mama found out it was Wynter Williams that had left food on her porch when she and the girls were hungry and alone, before she had left her first husband. Wynter Williams and his best friend, Big Don Buttram – Don Butt, to you and me.

I decided to stage a stakeout, like I'd seen on TV. If Don Butt came to Meyer's Grocery every week or two, then I'd be waiting for him. Every morning, I'd leave the house by 8:00 and ride my bike to Meyer's, which was in downtown Weir, across the east-west tracks and only a few minutes from my house. Meyer's was on Front Street, which faced the north-south tracks. It was among a row of businesses, a hardware store and a junk shop and a pool hall. Down further, there was a fancy clothing store and a hotel, but this part of Front Street was mostly downscale places. Meyer's was the mom-and-pop shop where country folk came to trade. There was really a Mr. and Mrs. Meyer that ran it, and they opened the place at 9:00, so I was there each day when Mr. Meyer unlocked the front door. The first two days, I parked my bike outside and walked around the store, studying the aisles of food and knick-knacks, like I was taking inventory. The first day, Mrs. Meyer thought it was cute, so she just played along and asked me if there was anything she could help me with and what I thought about the row of candy jars and what brands of cereal they ought to stock. The next day, she was frustrated by me, and starting asking if I had any money and whether I was going to buy anything or not and did my mama know where I was. So the third day, I just rode my bike up and down Front Street, craning my neck toward Meyer's Store whenever I passed it and double-checking whenever I saw a dusty old pick-up parked out front as to who was driving it. I discovered something important in all this. Stake-outs are boring!

I started varying my route more and more, making blocks, looping all around downtown, trying not to miss driving by Meyer's at least every 10-15 minutes. I figured nobody could get into Meyer's and buy all their groceries and be out of there in 15 minutes, especially when they'd made a special trip into town and especially if they were a talker like Don Butt. I was thankful when Sunday came and Meyer's was closed to give me a day of rest, but then on Monday, I was back, rolling all over downtown Weir, swishing by Meyer's, barely even casting my eyes toward the store, feeling hopeless and a little deranged, when I heard something familiar. A roar of thunder. Not from the sky, but from the sidewalk. It was loud and full and happy. I turned my bike and looked back toward Meyer's Store. There, in the front, talking to a skinny man with a sunken face, was Don Butt, laughing his fool head off.

I raced my bike up to him and skidded on the brakes. He turned and looked at me with surprise, first with an expression that seemed like he was going to tell me what for since I'd nearly run into him, but then it turned back to pure pleasure. "God bless, if it isn't Billy Williams. How the hell are you, boy?"

Out of breath, I answered, "Good. I'm real good."

"How's your mama? Saw her the other day. Just as full of spit and vinegar, as ever."

"Yes sir, she's fine."

Don Butt turned to the skinny man, who looked like he wanted to get on about his business. "This here's Wynter Williams' boy. You 'member Wynter Williams, don't you? Tall fellow, had a farm out to Highway 169. Salt of the earth, he was. Salt of the earth! Best friend I ever did have."

The skinny man nodded his head but his expression said he could care less. "Listen here, Don," he said, his voice raspy and thin. "I've got to get to the hardware store. I'll see you later."

"Alright. Alright, then." Don Butt turned toward me. "I got to get some groceries for my old woman. You want to come give me a hand?"

"Sure."

When I walked into the store behind Don Butt, like a piece of him that fell off and was about blow away, Mrs. Meyer cut her eye toward me with suspicion.

"Howdy there, Mrs. Meyers!" Don Butt proclaimed, and like so many people I'd heard over the years, he mispronounced their name with an "s" at the end that didn't belong there. "You're lookin' like a ray of sunshine in a cloudy day."

Mrs. Meyer looked away from me and smiled at Don Butt. "Thank you, Mr. Buttram," she turned back toward me. "Is this boy bothering you?"

"Bothering me? No ma'am. This boy's Billy Williams. His daddy and me was best friends. He's here to help me do my trading. You don't mind, do you?"

She smiled at Don Butt again. "Of course not." Don picked up a basket and walked past her to the grocery aisles. As I followed past him, her smile turned to a smirk again and she gave me a "I'm keeping an eye on you, boy" look.

Don spent about fifteen minutes gathering up flour, sugar, corn meal, canned goods, and other staples. He filled up one basket and sent me to the front counter with it. Then started filling up another, all the time, talking and laughing about things that happened to him and my father.

"...so there we was, boxed in amongst all them copperheads, neither one of us with a gun or a knife or even a stick. So I said to your daddy, 'Wynter, I ain't about to stand here and be venomized by a bunch of no-account, slimy, sorry snakes.' And he said, 'Don, what the hell are you gonna do about it?'" Don Butt looked over at Mrs. Meyer and nodded. "Excuse my language, ma'am. I do get carried away." Mrs. Meyer nodded back. Don Butt looked down at me. "Now where was I?"

"Daddy asked you what you were gonna do."

"That's right! He said, 'What the... what the heck are you gonna do, Don?' And I said, 'I'm gonna run.' And your daddy looked me up and down and said, 'Don, you ain't run ten feet since you was knee-high to a tadpole.' And I said, 'Well, that may be true, but I ain't had no good reason to, either.' And the two of us, we shot out there like bats out of..." Don looked over at Mrs. Meyer, who was listening intently, and whispered. "Like bats out of Hades." He spoke the word "Hades" so softly I almost couldn't understand him. "Let me tell you, we were running so fast, them old copperheads were flopping around in the wake," and he flopped his arms around imitating the snakes blowing in the wind and laughed loud and hard. "Yes sir. We never went fishing back there again." Don paused and thought for a second. "At least, I don't recall that we did. If'n we did, we would have taken some firepower with us the next time."

Don Butt finished his shopping and checked out with Mrs. Meyer. I helped him carry the grocery sacks to the back of his pickup truck. He'd told a handful of stories while we shopped but none of them that connected with what I'd heard and seen at the remains of the Carasell house. Don was about to get in his truck and head back home without giving me a clue so I needed to do something quick.

"Well, young'un, I guess I'd better head back to the home-stead. Would you like me to give you a ride back to your house?"

"Sure." Maybe this was my chance. "Can I just put my bike in the back of the truck?"

"Of course. Let me help you."

Don Butt and I put the bike in the bed of the pickup truck, and I crawled into the passenger side of the cab. Don backed up and I thought I'd try something.

"Did you hear about the fire?"

"What fire? Your mama hasn't been trying to burn your place down again, has she?"

"No sir. There was a house burned down over in the Macon neighborhood."

"Yeah?"

"Do you want to see it?"

Don scrunched up his lips and thought for a second. "Well, reckon we could take a look."

So Don followed my directions to the Carasell house. I looked at Don as we drove up. His expression was hard to read. I didn't see any sparks in his eyes, as if he was recalling some ancient memory, but I also didn't see that twinkle of good humor that seem to be present with him most of the time. He seemed noticeably unemotional about the place.

"Looks like they done cleaned it up," he remarked.

I nodded my head. "It was a big mess when I first saw it."

"Terrible thing, fires. Our house burned down when I was a boy. We had to sleep in the barn until we could build a new place. My brother Andy got bad burnt all over the side of his body." Don rubbed his arm. "His arm always looked like elephant skin after that."

"Fellow that owned the place was named Carasell. You ever heard of him?"

"Nope. Never have."

"You ever know anyone else that lived over this way?"

Don rubbed his hand on his chin as he thought. "I can't rightly remember. Seem like there was..." And then I saw something strike in his brain for a second. A memory that came and bounced around between his ears, and then just as quickly as it came, it was dismissed. "...No, I don't think so."

Don Butt put the pickup in gear and headed back toward my house. If he did know something about the house and my father, he was hiding it. I knew we'd be back home for long, and I would miss my chance, so I'd tried something bold.

"Did my daddy ever get in trouble with the law?"

"With the law?" he proclaimed. "Your daddy? Not likely. He got me out of trouble a couple of times, but..." Again, Don Butt eyes swirled and he was searching his memories. "Well, there was that one thing."

"What thing?"

"That colored boy. He didn't exactly get in trouble with the law, but he could have."

"I think my mama told me this story," I prompted him. "The guy worked for him and he got in some trouble."

"That's right. Your daddy thought high of this boy. He didn't think what was happening to him was right. So he helped him hightail it out of town. When the sheriff came looking for him, your daddy just kept his mouth shut."

"When was that?"

"Ah, 'fore you were born. He'd been married to your mama for a couple of years I guess."

"Do you remember the black boy's name?"

We pulled up in front of my house.

"Ah, goodness, no. That was almost twenty years ago. My old brain is too full of cobwebs to remember stuff like that."

Don Butt got out of the truck cab and helped me get my bike out of the back.

"I need to get back to the house. You give your mama my regards and tell her I think about her all the time."

"Yes sir."

Don crawled back into the truck and rolled down the street. Dejected by the lack of facts I accumulated in such a drawn-out endeavor, I pushed my bike toward the front door. Suddenly, I heard Don's brakes creak, and I turned to see him looking back at me out of the passenger window.

"Lionel Summer!" he shouted. "That was the boy's name. Lionel Summer. Nearly forgot it. I guess something got through them old cobwebs," he said stroking his finger on the side of his head. "Take care!" And he was gone.

Chapter 8

Was Lionel Summer just another wild goose chase, like the ones that my daddy and Don Butt used to go on? Hard to say. But for now, it was the only clue I had.

Despite Don Butt's plea to give my mama his regards, I didn't tell her that I had seen him that day, or that he'd given me a ride home. I thought it might seem suspicious to ask about Don Butt one week, and then get a ride home from him the next one, when I hadn't seen or talked about him in a couple of years. I don't know what I thought Mama would think I was suspicious of, but I didn't want her to think too much about what I was doing at all.

While Mama was cooking dinner that night, I pulled the thin little Weir phone book out from under our lime green telephone and looked for the name "Summer." Strange, but I didn't find anyone with the last name of Summer that lived in Weir. I found a Summerall and a Summerhill, but no Summer. I checked all the little towns in our county that surrounded Weir, and none of them had a Summer. Finding Lionel Summer would not be as easy as looking him up in the phone book.

The next day, it rained. Buckets. "Cats and dogs," as my mama used to say. "A frog strangler." I stayed inside, watched one of the TV channels that wasn't showing Watergate, worked on piecing together a gondola in the lower left corner of Mama's puzzle, and tried not to think too much about my father or Don Butt or Lionel Summer. In the afternoon, while Mama watched *The Guiding Light*, I closed myself up in my bedroom and started looking through my old toy box. I had outgrown most of the stuff in there, but the name of Lionel had reminded me of the train set I'd gotten a couple of years earlier. It was a big scale set on a figure-8 track, with an engine that looked like a steam train. It was not nearly as cool as the one Jim had gotten a few months later. His was smaller, sleeker and looked like a modern passenger train, like those sets you see on TV where some collector has built a whole town—stores and houses and cardboard trees—to go with it. Jim was always doing that to me. I'd get something new, something neither one of us had, and then on Christmas or his next birthday, or whatever, he'd get something that was twice as cool as what I had. I loved playing with Jim, but sometimes he could be a real pain.

I assembled the train tracks in the floor of my room and carefully lined up the railway cars, snapping one to the other. Only one thing was missing. The transformer that plugged into the tracks on one end and the wall socket on the other. I dug through the toy chest looking for the transformer, dumping stuffed animals and toy soldiers onto my bed. I came to a plastic bucket that held my Matchbox and Hot Wheels cars. Maybe I'd put the transformer in the car bucket. I opened the bucket and sorted through the cars until I came to one that was very ordinary but important.

It was a Ford Galaxie. A miniature version of the big 4-door sedan my father had bought when my mother was pregnant with me. Even though my parents had not planned to have a child, my father was excited at the prospect of a son with the woman he loved more than anything. My father had a pickup truck, but he worried about carrying my mother wouldn't be comfortable riding in a pickup truck to the hospital. Mama gave it no thought; frankly, she'd never had a child at a hospital. Her older children had all been born at home with the help of a midwife, but Daddy didn't like that thought. Perhaps it was because my mother was in her mid-40s and he thought she might have trouble with the delivery. Perhaps he just wanted to be modern and take her to the brand new hospital in Weir, like so many folks were doing now. Perhaps it was just an excuse to buy a car. Regardless, he bought the Ford Galaxie for Mama, even though she couldn't drive it and didn't give a hoot. When one of my sisters saw the Matchbox version of the Galaxie, she just had to get it for me, and here it was in my hand.

I had a few memories of the Galaxie. It was the car Papa was driving when he let me sit on his lap and steer. I can remember driving around town in the Galaxie. He would tell me stories, most of which I can't remember, about what he did when he was a boy. We would drive all over the county and all over Weir in that beautiful old car.

When he died, his oldest daughter's husband Arthur took it, since Mama couldn't drive. Figured it was his inheritance. Since Papa didn't leave a will, dividing up the property became a free-for-all. Thank goodness Mama had dowry rights to his property or we would have had everything, including the farm, pulled out from under us. The argument for keeping the Galaxie was not a good one, and she let it go to Arthur. A year or two later, we heard that Arthur had burned the car up. Didn't bother to change the oil or do anything to keep up with it. Mama cried. She couldn't drive the car, but it still felt like hers.

I took the little Galaxie and placed it on my dresser. I couldn't find the transformer for the train, so I packed the whole thing up and put it back in the toy box. Everything I did and saw was drawing me toward my father. But I needed some assurance that the route I was taking made sense. Perhaps this voice I heard and this feeling I had was just my imagination. I needed to return to where this all began. To the scene of the crime, you might say.

The rain subsided the next day. It was still wet outside, but that made riding your bike even more fun. You could zoom through puddles and spray water to both sides. The roads were slick so when you hit your brakes, you'd slide. Best of all, it cooled the place down. It was June in Arkansas, and we'd had 90-degree temperatures every day. The rain had made the summer weather nearly tolerable.

As I sped down Maple Street on the way to the Carasell house, I slowed down in front of Mabel Ann's place. I half expected to see her and Groucho playing in the front yard. Mabel Ann was the only person I entrusted with knowledge of this, and it would feel good to talk to her about what I had found out. But neither she nor her little mutt were anywhere around. They were probably keeping dry inside the house. I just wasn't brave enough to go to the door and knock. That would be too obvious.

There's a little creek that runs through the Macon neighborhood, and as I crossed the bridge over it, I almost stopped to take a look. The rain from the day before had turned it into a raging river. I loved playing around creeks and drainage ditches and anywhere there was water flowing. You could watch sticks flow down it and skip rocks across it and jump over it and try not to get wet and fall in anyway. No boy could resist a creek.

"Hey, Billy!" I heard crying out from behind me. I hit my brakes and slid on the slick asphalt. When I turned I saw Mabel Ann coming toward me from down the creek. She had Groucho in her hands.

"Hey," I said out of breath.

"Where're you going in such a hurry? Oh, let me guess."

"What are you doing out here?" I asked.

"I was taking Groucho for a walk. He was bored from all the rain yesterday."

"Looks like Groucho's taking you for a walk."

"He got tired. Can I come with you?"

I tried to hold back my enthusiasm as much as I could. "Sure."

I got off my bike and walked beside Mabel Ann.

"Have you been back here since the other day?" she asked.

"No. Well, I did come by with a friend, but we never got out of his truck."

"So you hadn't heard any more voices?"

"No. I've only heard the voices here. How about you?"

"Oh, I hear voices all the time," she said. "I'm kind of bored of them."

"Is it always your father?"

"No. Different voices. Different people. Someone always seems to have something to say to me."

As we walked toward the place where the Carasell house had stood, I told Mabel Ann about my search for Don Butt and about

Lionel Summer and how my father protected him, even though it was something he shouldn't have done.

"So what makes you think that any of that has anything to do with this house and hearing your father's voice?"

"A hunch, I guess. It had to be something serious from the way he sounded."

"I think you're trying to make too much sense out of this. It was your father's voice. He said something kind of scary. What else is it that you need to know?"

"I need to know why my father sounded so..."

"Scared?"

"Mean... Angry... What was happening to him?"

"So you don't think this was your father's ghost talking to you directly? You think it was some flashback, like on TV, to something that happened in the past."

"Yeah. What else could it be?"

"What did he say?"

"Put that down. And he said it really seriously, more than once."

"So how do you know he wasn't talking to you?"

"I didn't have anything in my hand. I didn't have anything to put down. And my daddy wouldn't talk to me like that."

"Your daddy didn't live long enough to talk to you like that. All daddies get angry. All daddies talk tough."

I shut up. Maybe she was right. Maybe he was talking to me. Maybe this had nothing to do with the past. But it still didn't make sense. Why would my father's ghost only speak to me at this place? And why would he tell me something so impossible to understand? If my father had something he needed so desperately to tell me from beyond the grave, why didn't he just come out and say it? Why does everything have to be such a damn puzzle? Couldn't somebody at least sort out the edge pieces for me?

"Here we are," declared Mabel Ann as we walked up to the vacant lot where the Carasell house had once stood. I realized I had never actually seen the house itself, only its burned out remnants. Mabel Ann put Groucho on the ground and he ran right to the middle of the concrete slab and started barking. "Maybe he hears HIS daddy," Mabel Ann joked.

"Stop making fun of me!" I declared, dropping my bike and marching toward the slab.

I plopped down on the slab and lowered my head. Mabel Ann came and sat down beside me. "I'm sorry," she whispered. "I'm not used to someone being as messed-up as me." Groucho came up to me and started licking on my face. I tried to look away from him, but he was persistent. Eventually, I couldn't help but start to laugh. Mabel Ann began laughing, too. The next thing I knew, the two of us were rolling around on the ground, trying to avoid getting licked.

"Hey!" a strong voice cried out. I froze. Was it my dad? "Hey, what are you kids doing here?"

I looked up from the ground. It was no disembodied voice. It was from a man standing at the edge of the street. He was about 30, with thick, unkempt hair, and lips that were tightly pursed. Groucho was unaffected by the man's presence. He continued jumping around and barking at us. Mabel Ann sat up straight and looked right at the man.

"Playing with our dog. What are you doing here?"

"What am I...?" The man came marching toward us. Mabel Ann grabbed Groucho and held him tight as the hairy, scruffy man towered over us. "This is my property. That's what I'm doing here."

I stood up. "Mr. Carasell?" I asked without hesitation.

"That's right." Carasell turned his head sideways. "How do you know my name?"

"I just knew the house that burned down was owned by Mr. Justin Carasell."

"That's right. People are sure nosey in this town."

Mabel Ann stood up. "People are just concerned about their neighbors in this town."

"Well, they're not concerned about people's private property, are they?" Carasell's eyes flipped back and forth between me and Mabel Ann. "You kids need to clear off my property." Groucho made a little whelp. "And take this mangy dog with you."

"He is not mangy," Mabel Ann protested. "I just gave him a bath yesterday."

"Well, maybe you're the mangy one then."

Mabel Ann rolled her eyes and walked past Carasell. After she passed him, she turned and stuck her tongue out at him. It was hard for me to keep from laughing. I followed her away from Carasell, who stepped up onto the slab and examined the place his house once stood.

I stopped and turned toward him. "Did you live here, Mr. Carasell?" I asked.

Carasell turned abruptly toward me. "No," he barked. "Not that it's any of your business. It's a rental property. I inherited it from my uncle. I live in a real city."

"Nashville?"

"That's right. Nashville." Carasell drew a shallow breath. "You are one nosey kid."

"I want to be a newspaper reporter one day."

"Well, you're cut just about right for that."

"What are you going to do now?"

Carasell looked around his vacant lot.

"Wait." He sat down on the slab. "There's an investigation. Once that's finished, hopefully, I can collect the insurance."

"An investigation? How come?"

"You don't know. Well, that's surprising."

Carasell seemed a little friendlier now, so I walked toward him. "Do they think it's arson?"

"Worse than that. They think I burned it down myself."

"For the insurance money?"

Carasell pulled a cigarette out of his pocket and began lighting up. "Yeah. Place had been vacant for six months. Wasn't worth much anyway, and a real pain to rent out." Carasell took a deep drag on the cigarette. "The cops wanted to talk to me about it. That's why I'm here." Carasell looked right at me and smiled. "You're not an undercover cop, are you?"

"No." I pointed behind me with my thumb. "But she might be."

Carasell looked at Mabel Ann, who stood with Groucho, near the sidewalk. He laughed so hard he started to cough. "That's a good one." He pulled the pack of cigarettes back out of his pocket. "You want one?"

"No thanks."

"Clean arrow, huh?"

"Mostly."

Carasell put away the cigarettes and leaned back on his elbows. "So what else you want to know, kid? It's your dime."

"How long have you owned this place?"

"Mmmm... about four or five years."

"And your uncle owned it before that?"

"Right."

"What was his name?"

"Balls."

"Balls?"

"First name, Harry."

I put the two together and smirked. Carasell laughed big and coughed again.

"Naw, really kid. His name was Harry. Harry Maxwell."

"Did anyone else own it before him?"

"Don't know. Don't care." Carasell took another deep drag on his cigarette.

"What was he like?"

"Who?"

"Your uncle."

"I don't know. He was just an uncle. Saw him maybe once a year. At Thanksgiving. He died without any kids. That's why I ended up with this house. Are you about finished with the interrogation?"

"Yeah. Thanks."

"Don't mention it."

"I hope you get your money."

"Me, too, kid. Thanks."

I turned and walked toward my bike.

"This is your last warning."

I turned back toward Carasell. "What did you say?"

Carasell was blowing smoke rings. "I didn't say nothing, kid."

"You sure?"

"Positive. Are you losing it?"

"Maybe."

I met Mabel Ann at my bike. She whispered. "Did you hear something?"

I picked up my bike. "Yeah."

"Was it your dad?"

"I don't think so."

We started walking away. "Now you've really got problems. You're starting to sound like me."

Chapter 9

As we continued down the sidewalk, we heard the roar of a car coming behind us. We turned to see Carasell barrel past us in a Gran Torino. He gave us a quick brush of his hand that was either a wave or the finger.

"What a jerk!" Mabel Ann proclaimed. "Do you think he burned down his house?"

"Could be. I guess the cops'll figure it out if he did."

"So what did the voice say?"

I studied on it for a second. "This is your last warning."

"That sounds serious. Who'd it sound like?"

"Nobody I know."

Mabel Ann turned toward me. "You look kind of scared."

"I am."

"How come?"

"When I heard my father's voice, even though it was kind of eerie, it was comforting, too. This voice, though, this voice... I don't know what to think."

"Do you think the voice was talking to you directly?"

"I don't know."

"Was it talking to your dad?"

"I don't know."

"What do you think it means?"

"I don't know!"

Mabel Ann finally got the message and shut up. I walked with her silently back to her place and then gave her a wave and took off on my bike, riding back to my house. I pedaled faster and faster, and as I did, my mind focused in on that phrase: "This is your last warning." "This is your LAST warning." Every time my right foot pedaled down, I heard the word "Last." "This is your LAST warning." The speaker, whoever he was, couldn't be addressing me. I hadn't gotten a first warning. I was convinced that my dad saying, "Put that down," was not addressed to me, and besides, it was not my dad who said, "This is your last warning." It was someone else. Someone talking TO my dad.

As I rolled down Jefferson Street to my house, I saw some kids from the neighborhood who had set up a crash course. It was Mark Twilley, Ronnie Rodgers and Laura Kindren, the girl who used to throw rocks at me from across the street. They'd piled some old wooden planks on a stack of cinder blocks so they could race their bikes up the ramp and make jumps like Evel Knieval. He was every boy's hero, a stunt driver who fearlessly jumped his motorcycle over increasingly longer distances. He'd jumped over 19 cars, a world record, a few years before, but he'd also missed a couple of jumps since then and found himself laid up in the hospital. Part of his appeal was that he kept trying, even when he failed. You'd hear about Evel Knieval getting cracked ribs and a broken hip, and then a few months later, you'd hear about his next exploit. He dreamed of jumping the Grand Canyon, but the U.S. Government did not want any part of that.

In honor of Knieval, Mark and Ronnie had placed some toy cars on the other side of their ramp. Laura, a real flirt, was sitting on the ground watching them. She seemed less interested in jumping than trying to get the boys' attention by cheering them on. Mark and Ronnie were studying their course when I rode up.

"Hey, Billy," Ronnie shouted to me. "You want to try our ramp?"

I stopped my bike and looked at it. "Is it safe?"

"Safe? Sure it is. I built it myself."

"I found the cinder blocks," Mark interjected.

"Yeah, but I stacked them."

I studied it myself for a while. It looked fun, but it made me nervous. I didn't mind a little scrape here and there from trying some stunt, but that looked like brain damage. I turned to the two boys, "Have you tried it?"

"Not yet," answered Ronnie. "We're sizing it up."

"One of you try it first," I suggested. "Show me how it's done. Then I'll give it a try."

"What are you?" Mark sneered. "A scaredy-cat?"

The term "scaredy-cat" almost got to me. I did not want to be thought of as a "scaredy-cat," even if I was one. But I didn't take Mark's bait. "You built it. You show me how it's done. Or are you a scaredy-cat?"

Mark, on the other hand, could not take being called a "scaredy-cat." "I'll show you," he declared.

Mark lined up his bike, while Ronnie backed away from him. He got this serious look on his face, like I imagined Evel Knieval looked underneath his helmet visor. Of course Mark wasn't wearing a visor or a helmet or any protective gear. Just cut-offs and a greasy T-shirt. Ronnie gave him some encouraging words, and Mark got down low to his bike and began pedaling, hard and fast. He rolled right up to the wooden plank, but he didn't quite hit it straight on. Instead, he slid to the side and the plank went the other direction. He rolled off his bike and flew almost into Laura Kindren's lap.

Ronnie and I rode up to him, and he was cursing and spitting, while Laura stroked his head.

"Ah, you poor thing, are you okay?" She seemed to be in heaven.

"I told you we should've gotten a wider plank!" Mark yelled at Ronnie.

"Maybe you ought to try it the first time with one block instead of two."

Ronnie looked at me and nodded his head. "I think I know where I can find a wider plank," and Ronnie sped away on his bike while Mark continued rolling around on the ground with Laura comforting him.

"Good luck," I said and continued on to my house.

By the time I got to my front yard, I had become convinced that I was only a witness and not part of the drama I had experienced at the Carasell place. I was not being haunted by my father, but by something that happened to him, something long ago before I was born. I had believed this from the first day I visited the Carasell house, and now I was convinced. If I had any role in this story, it was to discover what happened and understand why this piece of history wouldn't die. Whether Lionel Summer was a part of it or not, I couldn't say, but I became fairly certain that Harry Maxwell was a key player. And if Harry Maxwell was anything like his nephew, there was one person who might know something about him.

"Whatever happened to the sheriff who stood up for you in court?" I asked Mama that night at dinner.

"Sheriff Colby? Ah, he retired about ten years ago. I think he's in a nursing home."

"Which one?"

"Goodness, I don't know. There's only about two or three in town. Why you want to know?"

Finally, I came up with an answer that would cover many bases. "I heard we had to write our autobiography in sixth grade, so I was just wanting to do some research over the summer." It was true. Every sixth grader in Weir Junior High had to write an autobiography. I don't think many of them did research though.

"Ain't you got enough studying to do during the school year without stretching it into summer vacation?"

Mama didn't disvalue education. She just didn't understand it. She'd only made it through third grade. Her mother made her quit school and stay home to take care of her younger brothers and sisters while she worked in the fields. Mama could read and write, although not very legibly, but her math skills were sorely lacking. She had to have someone else, usually one of my older sisters, balance her checkbook for her. Later, I would do it. She did have one outstanding math skill. She could add up all the little dots on dominoes in her head in seconds and proclaim her score with some pretended uncertainty: "I think that's 45 points." She was the domino champion of our family.

We discussed for a while that my preparation for classes in the fall was valuable, and she accepted it. She did warn me that I shouldn't be bothering people with a lot of questions. It was always best to keep your mouth shut and avoid making people angry. I basically agreed, but in this instance, I saw the need to work a little outside my comfort zone.

The next day I began visiting nursing homes. The reaction of having an 11-year-old boy walk into a nursing home and ask to see one of the patients was quite varied. At the first place, I visited the woman in the front thought it was very nice that a young man would be coming to visit an old fellow who wasn't even his grandpa. At the second nursing home, they looked at me suspiciously, wondering if I was going to cause a ruckus or try to steal something. When they told me Jeremiah Colby was not a patient there, I wasn't really sure whether they were telling the truth or not. At the third nursing home, I was met with a shrug. I had walked up and down the halls a couple of times before I found anyone in authority that would talk to me. When I finally did find someone, it was an orderly, changing out bedding. I asked about Jeremiah Colby, and he scratched his head and pointed a couple of times without saying anything. Finally, he answered, "Room 342," and I took off.

Outside of Room 342 was a sign that said "J. Colby and R. Godfrey." Inside the room, I found two men. One was sitting in a rocking chair, staring out the window and whistling. The other one was in his bed, softly moaning. Quietly, I asked, "Sheriff Colby?"

Fortunately, it was the whistler sitting by the window who turned and greeted me. "That's me."

Mr. Godfrey moaned again, and I turned to look at him. "Ah, don't mind Roscoe there. He's not really hurting. Just tired of being in that bed. Look there." He pointed to Mr. Godfrey's hands, which were tied to his bed. "They have to tie him down or he'd go wandering out in the street. Caught him one time when he'd made it all the way to Ridge Road. Poor thing looked peaked and worn. Funny though. He was happy as a clam. Nothing like freedom. So young man, what are you doing here?"

I explained to Sheriff Colby I was working on a project for school. Like my mother, he was shocked that I'd be doing school-work during the summer, so I told him it was a special assignment that would get me some extra credit next year.

"What kind of assignment is this?"

"Well, it's kind of a history. Of the Macon neighborhood."

"Macon, huh? Why would anybody want to know about that place?"

"Well, we're all getting different places around town to study, and Macon's the one I drew."

"Macon. Alright. What do you want to know?"

"There was a name I ran across, and someone told me you might know this person."

"Okay."

"Harry Maxwell."

"Oh my God, yes. Harry Maxwell. I hadn't heard that name in a while."

A little swell of excitement rushed through me. "What can you tell me about him?"

"Gosh-durn, boy. He wasn't nothing but an old gambler. Cheating people out of their hard-earned money every chance he got."

Harry Maxwell ran a floating crap game that Sheriff Colby chased after for years. He would set up a place to play for a while, like in the back of the hardware store, over in a house on 7th Street, or down by the cotton gin, and move on when he thought the police were closing in on him. Sheriff Colby had arrested him two or three times, but he never gave it up.

"He had a bookmaking racket, too. You know what that is?"

The sheriff explained that Harry would take bets over the phone, usually on races at Oaklawn Park in Hot Springs, then hire some thug to make collections for him. He had one fellow who worked the white side of town, and a black guy who worked on the other side of the tracks.

"I remember one of them colored boys that worked for him. His name was Cletus. He was about 6-foot-4, weighed 250 pounds, scary as all get out. I had to take him in one time. I had lots of backup from the city cops."

"Did you know," I asked, "that Harry Maxwell's place over in Macon burned down a few weeks ago."

"Do tell. That little white frame house on Pickman. He didn't really live there. Usually kept it for his thugs. The city police raided it a couple of times. Disorderly conduct, disturbing the peace, and guess what? Gambling."

"Do you miss it? Chasing the bad guys."

"Course, I do. You think I like sitting in this rocking chair, listening to old Roscoe moan all day long? But I got the cancer a few years ago, and I'm lucky to be alive. Et up quite a bit of my insides before it let go. Doctor says it's gone for now, but don't put too much faith in it. I could be zip... gone tomorrow."

"Do you remember my mother? Her name was Juniper Evans. Now it's Williams."

"Juniper Evans? Oh, yeah. She had one mean husband. Ran that boy out of town on a rail. Good riddance." Sheriff Colby caught himself. "That wasn't your dad, was it?"

"No sir. My father was Wynter Williams. He died about seven years ago."

"Wynter Williams... Oh, I recollect him. A farmer."

"My mother was telling me a story about a black man who worked for him. His name was Lionel Summer."

"Summer? I don't recollect any colored folk named Summer that lived around here."

I nodded my head and thanked Sheriff Colby for his help.

"Did you get enough stories about the old days to suit you?"

"Yes sir."

Mr. Godfrey moaned loud when I turned to walk out the door. "Roscoe says thanks for coming by."

I made my way down the hall and past several employees, none of whom paid me any mind. I was at the front door when I heard Sheriff Colby's voice. "Boy, hold on." He walked up to me, breathing hard.

"Yes sir?"

"It wasn't Summer. It was Sumner. There was a whole bunch of Sumners living over in colored town. Lionel must have been one of them. I don't remember him specifically, but that must be who you're talking about."

I nodded my head. "Thank you, Sheriff. Are you okay?"

Still breathing hard. "Fine. Fine. Lungs just don't work quite as good as they used to." He turned and shuffled back down the hall.

Chapter 10

When I got back to the house, I pulled out the phone book and looked for the name Sumner. Sure enough, there was three Sumners listed for Weir. I don't know why I didn't look past Summerhill to see that. Poor old Don Butt just didn't quite have it right. The three names listed were A. J. Sumner, M. M. Sumner and R. L. Sumner. Their addresses were all streets I didn't recognize so I guessed they were on the other side of the tracks. If one of them was Lionel, my best guess would be R. L., thinking maybe Lionel was his middle name. Of course, he might not be any of them. He might be dead. But surely one of these people was kin to him and would know what become of him.

I almost never made phone calls. When Jim was living across the street, I used to call him on school nights to talk for a while before we went to bed. Now that he had moved, Mama would let me call him long distance on Sunday nights once a month. The longer Jim had been gone, the longer the stretch between those phone calls, and I hardly called him at all now. I'd called my sisters once or twice, when I wanted to tell them what I wanted for my birthday. I called one of my teachers one time when I forgot an assignment. If I was to make a phone call, Mama would want to know who I was calling and why. The autobiography excuse just wouldn't hold much water in this case.

I decided to wait until Mama was out of the house. This took patience. Mama didn't leave the house except once a week to go downtown to the store, and if I was home, she'd make me go with her to carry her sacks. I had to mount another stakeout. Only this time, the stakeout was on my own house.

I figured if I told Mama I was going riding, and she went to town later that day, I could hide out and wait until she left, then go in the house and make some calls. Only problem—Mama locked the place when she left and I didn't have a key. I'd been locked out of the place before, coming back to the house to pee and finding Mama gone. I had to make do with a tree in the backyard. I can attest, it wasn't as bad as using an outhouse.

If I was to get back in the house, I'd have to come up with some strategy. There was no hidden key that I knew of. My sister Layla, who lived across town, had one, but I couldn't think of any good excuse for getting a key from her that wouldn't raise suspicion. Mama was extra special careful about checking all the locks so trying to set one door so it wouldn't lock was out. I thought about leaving a window unlocked so I could crawl inside after she was gone, but Mama was just ticky enough that she'd probably check the windows, too. I don't know why she was so careful about locking the place up. It wasn't like we had anything much to steal. Finally, I decided the only way to get back in the house was never to leave it in the first place.

I made my play the morning Mama said we were about out of bread. I knew she'd head out later that day to the store. After breakfast, I told her I was going to ride my bike up to Saratoga Hills and she wished me a good day. I rode the bike around the block to a bushy area behind our house and hid it there. Then I snuck back to our house and watched Mama through the kitchen window, where she was washing dishes in the sink. When she left the window, I got closer to the back door and listened. I heard her close the bathroom door and made my play.

Fortunately, she'd left the wood door open and the screen door unhooked. As quietly as I could, I came through the screen door. The screen door creaked a little so sneaking through it was not easy. When I got inside, I made straight for the pantry and closed the door behind me. At the back of our pantry was a staircase that led up to the attic. There was nothing in our attic at all. Mama didn't like going up there. It was dusty and she didn't like climbing stairs, so it was a place that was pretty much off limits. The pantry stairs had always given me a bit of a scare. It was just creepy walking into the place where you stored your canned goods and cleaning supplies and finding a staircase leading up into the darkness. Now, here I was, carefully climbing those stairs in the dark, trying to keep my footsteps quiet, and avoid my mother. If she caught me, I don't know who'd be more scared— her or me.

As I reached the top of the stairs, I heard the pantry door open and the light flipped on. I froze. Mama walked into the pantry and studied the shelves. At my position on the staircase, she couldn't see me so I just stayed as still as I could. She was only there for a few seconds, but it seemed like an eternity. She flipped off the light and exited. I listened and heard her lock the back door. Then I heard the sound in the distance of the front door being locked. I flew down the stairs and out the pantry door. I tiptoed around the house, still thinking she might be there and inspected every corner. No Mama nowhere.

I sat down at the telephone and looked up the phone number for R. L. Sumner. What would I say if he answered? Mr. Sumner, do you remember my daddy? What did he do for you? Have you ever been to Harry Maxwell's house in Macon? Do you think I'm crazy?

I dialed the number. It rang three times, and then the voice of young boy came on the line. "Hello?"

"Hello, does Lionel Sumner live there?"

"Yes."

"May I speak to him please."

"You're speaking to him."

"Lionel Sumner?"

"Yep."

"How old are you?"

"Eight. How old are you?"

I stuttered around for a second. "Um, eleven."

"What do you want?"

"Is there another Lionel Sumner there?"

"No." I started to hang up when the boy's voice came on again. "He's at work. Do you want to speak to my mama?"

"No, no. Where's he work?"

"At the shoe factory. He usually gets off about 3:00 o'clock. You got anything else you want?"

"No. Thank you." And I hung up.

So I got my answer. There was a Lionel Sumner that lived right here in Weir. In fact, there were two of them. And he worked at the shoe factory. And he got off at 3:00. So what was I going to do about it? I made my way back to the pantry and up the stairs to wait for Mama to come back. I'd have to wait until she unloaded all the groceries in the pantry, hiding in the shadows of the attic, before I could go retrieve my bike and make it look like I'd been off enjoying myself in the outdoors. Richard Nixon sure made my summer pretty awful.

Chapter 11

You need to know that I was not a deceitful kid. I didn't usually hide from my mother and avoid telling the truth. Or just plain lie, for that matter. I was usually honest with my mother and shy around other adults. The voices, however, had driven me to turn away from my normal behavior and adopt a method I'd experienced first-hand somewhere else—on television.

TV was full of detectives, who would snoop around and lie and do whatever they could to find out what they needed to know. There were tough guys like McGarrett on *Hawaii Five-O* and *Mannix*. Then there were cops who played it more by the book, like Karl Malden and Michael Douglas on *The Streets of San Francisco* and Raymond Burr on *Ironside*. Then there were quirky characters like McCloud, a cowboy trying to make it as a detective in the big city; the immense Cannon, the fattest detective on TV; and of course, Columbo, sloppy and stumbling, but always smarter than the crooks he was trying to catch. And then there was *The Mod Squad*, three undercover cops—Pete, Julie and Linc—who were hippies. If these guys could solve crimes, so could I.

Of course, I really didn't have a crime I was investigating. Just a mystery. One that involved ghosts, or something like ghosts. Maybe I should have turned away from prime time television to Saturday morning cartoons and drawn my inspiration from Scooby Doo and the gang in the Mystery Machine. If that was the case, I would have eventually discovered that the voices were generated by some nefarious character (probably Justin Carasell) for the purpose of scaring away anybody that got in the way of his plan to collect a treasure. Unfortunately, that sounded a lot more plausible than the direction I was headed. I just didn't think Carasell was smart enough to pull off something like that. "I would have gotten away with it, too, if it hadn't been for you meddling kids!"

Instead, I put my hard-nosed detective work toward trying to catch up with Lionel Sumner. I had his street address, but I was still nervous about crossing the tracks, and I wouldn't know where to go once I got there. I decided another stakeout was in order, at the shoe factory.

The Roseman Shoe Factory was one of the main employers in Weir. Hundreds of people were on duty 24 hours a day, assembling shoes and sending them off to some distributor somewhere. Several of my friends' parents had worked there over the years. I knew there were three shifts: 7:00 a.m. to 3:00 p.m., 3:00 p.m. to 11:00 p.m., and 11:00 p.m. to 7:00 a.m. Somehow, Lionel Sumner had scored the day shift. Maybe he'd worked there a long time and had seniority. Maybe the workers traded shifts around. I knew the shifts but I didn't know how the schedules worked.

Like everything in Weir, the Roseman Shoe Factory was not far from my house, so I rode out there at about 2:30. People were already pulling into the parking lot for the 3:00 o'clock shift when I got there. I figured I was safe. While the workers starting at 3:00 might get there early, I didn't figure there was any circumstance in which the 7:00 to 3:00 shift would get off early. I parked my bike under a tree in a vacant lot across the street from the factory and started my lookout. People continued streaming into the factory for the next thirty minutes, but then suddenly, dozens of people began pouring out. Many of them headed straight for their cars and drove away. Others left on foot. A group of a dozen or so black men bunched together and walked toward the railroad tracks to the west. On a hunch, I decided to follow them.

At first I pedaled my bike, but they were walking so slow, I kept having to hit the brakes. Finally, I got off my bike and walked it. The men were laughing and talking about their shifts and about what they would do later that day. I wasn't really paying attention to what they were talking about, but rather names. I heard James, Samuel, Leroy, but no Lionel. Soon the men were at the railroad tracks and crossing to the other side. I could have followed, but I already looked suspicious following a group of black men. I'd look downright obvious walking my bike behind them over the tracks. I leaned my bike against a stop sign and plopped down on the ground to think.

"You alright, son?" I looked up to see a black man standing above me. He was tall and dark and had a pink scar on his temple.

"Yes sir," I responded automatically.

"Look like something's bothering you. Nobody messing with you, is there?"

"No, sir. I'm alright." I decided to take a chance. "You work at the shoe factory?"

"Sure do. Have now for seven year."

"Do you know a fellow named Lionel?"

"Maybe. Depend on why you want to know."

"I think he was a friend of my father's."

"Oh, you do. Who was your father?"

"Wynter Williams."

The man's face lit up. "Wynter Williams? You Wynter Williams' boy."

"Yes sir."

"Well, I'll be. Why you looking for Lionel? What's he done?"

"I just want to ask him about a story I heard."

"Story about what?"

"Something that happened a long time ago."

"I tell you what, young man. You meet me here tomorrow at this same time, and I'll bring Lionel to see you."

"Okay. Thanks."

I watched the black man as he crossed the tracks. I was getting ready to mount my bike and head back home when I heard a tapping noise. Maybe a woodpecker. I looked around and saw an old lady standing inside her house and knocking on the window. When she saw that she'd gotten my attention, she motioned for me to come to her. I left my bike at the side of the road and walked to the house. The old lady opened the window.

"What you doing, boy, talking to that Negro?"

"Just talking, ma'am."

"You need to be careful. I watch 'em everyday, coming by here. I know what they're up to. Looking for stuff to steal."

"I think they're just going back and forth to work." I pointed. "At the factory over there."

"Work, hah! I don't believe that. Worthless. Just a bunch of thieves. I keep my stuff locked up." Her eyes darted above my head. "There's another one."

I turned to see another black man walk past the intersection and toward the tracks. He didn't look toward us, but as he walked past my bike, he looked down at it without stopping.

"There, see. Just trying to steal your bicycle. That's all they want from you. You better get home and stay away from this part of town, if you know what's good for you." The old lady nodded her head with a "humph" and slammed shut the window, making sure she twisted the lock.

I turned back toward the road and wondered if she really did stare out the window all day long, watching the blacks pass by her house. It must have been a constant occupation.

I picked up my bike and headed south toward my home. I wondered if anybody would really want my old bike. It was well worn. I'd had it for three or four years. The paint was starting to chip off of it. If it got stolen, all the better. It would be a good excuse to get one of those ten-speeds.

That night, I lay in bed thinking about my father. The streetlight next to our house cast a glow on the Matchbox Ford Galaxie I'd set on my dresser. Next to it, I'd placed the toy combine my dad and Don Butt had searched all over town for. It was shoved under my bed with a couple of other farm toys—a John Deere tractor like my dad owned and a backhoe. I wondered what my dad might say to me if he was there that night. Probably, "Go to sleep." He was a man of few words.

Chapter 12

It would be 3:00 o'clock before I could meet Lionel at the crossroads, and I couldn't concentrate on television. Just as well. The networks were back to wall-to-wall Watergate on all three channels. John Dean was testifying, and everyone seemed assured that whatever he had to say would answer a lot of questions. My mother grunted. "They're all a bunch of liars and cheats. They all ought to go to prison." And when she said "all," I think she meant politicians in general. The ones answering questions and the ones asking them, too. Mama had little respect for politicians, especially the ones on TV. She'd never voted in her life. Said it was useless. The truth is, she was afraid if she registered to vote, she'd be called up for jury duty. That idea scared her to death. She'd spent a lot of years watching Perry Mason, and unless Perry was there to tell her what to do, she'd be lost.

I took off on my bike to the Carasell place, or I guess maybe I should say, the Maxwell house. Of course, when I thought of it as the Maxwell House, all I could think of was "good to the last drop." So I just stuck with Carasell.

I took a route that avoided going past Mabel Ann's house. I was hoping to hear something new or experience a different feeling than I'd had before, and I thought it would be easier to do that if I was alone. Mabel Ann had kept me from being so scared when I visited the Carasell place before, but I was beginning to get braver, and I thought I would be fine.

I rolled up to the concrete slab and slid off my bike. I wondered if anyone in the neighborhood around there had noticed my coming here so often. They might call the police. But then again, kids were always congregating around vacant lots and empty buildings, anywhere that grown-ups were not. I especially liked to find construction sites on weekends when all the workers were gone. It was exciting walking through a half-built house, being able to see where the pipes and the wires ran and imagine what the place would look like when it was done. Mr. Reynolds had gotten me interested in construction. He had built a couple of apartments next to our house, and I got to watch the process all the way through. From mixing concrete and laying cinder blocks to shingling the roof and finishing the trim inside. Now whenever I saw a house being built, I would venture inside it and rate the progress for myself. It was a lot more fascinating than this slab of concrete where a house had once stood. All you could really do was guess where the walls had stood, and find the busted pipes that would have connected to toilets and sinks now long gone.

I sat down and closed my eyes, thinking if I concentrated, I could bring the voices to life. I sat there for who knows how long until a voice finally pierced through the chirp of crickets and the bellow of an old horny toad.

"Do you live here now?"

I opened my eyes, half-expecting to see the ghost of Harry Maxwell. Instead, it was Dewey Barnes.

"Hey, Dewey," I said, trying to pretend I was happy to see him.

"The only place I see you anymore is here. What have you been doing?"

What had I been doing? What a question! "Nothing. What have you been doing?"

Dewey sat down next to me. "Nothing. Just riding my bike." Dewey picked his nose but tried to make it look like he was just scratching it. "Hey, I found a tree that got struck by lightning the other day. You remember that storm?"

"Yeah."

"This tree got hit, and it's got the strangest looking carving in it. Like space aliens or something. You want to take a look at it?"

"Sure," I lied. I wanted to stay there and concentrate, but I couldn't while Dewey was yammering. He was a friend, and I couldn't blow him off again. I'd already done that twice before.

Dewey led me several blocks from the Carasell place to a field on the edge of town. There was a fence around the field and a line of trees along the fence, elms and oaks, just the kind of hardwoods you'd expect around here. We stopped at one tree that was black as soot with no leaves or branches.

"This is it," Dewey declared and jumped off his bike. I followed him to the tree, which had a huge scar from where the lightning had hit it. Some of the bark had fallen off and underneath were some mangled images. "Look close," Dewey said and pointed toward the images. "That one right there. It looks just like something from the movies." I bent over close, and sure enough, the figure seemed to have a bulbous head, big eyes, and thin, sharp lips. I couldn't say what movie I had seen with this creature, but I'd stayed up late on Saturday nights enough watching Sci Fi Theater to know a space alien when I saw one.

My face was almost right up to the tree when Dewey gave me a shove from behind. My face smacked into the tree, and I got the taste of charred wood in my mouth. Dewey was dying laughing. I turned on him, spitting burnt splinters from my mouth.

"What did you do that for?" I squealed.

"Just wanted to see if kissing that alien was as good as kissing old Mabel Ann McCarthy."

"I ain't never kissed Mabel Ann McCarthy."

"Well, you sure act like you like her."

"Naw I don't."

"That day I caught you two over at the burned-down house, you told me you were going to see what kind of crazy things she had to say and tell me about it. Then I never heard from you."

"I've been busy."

"Kissing on Mabel Ann. I bet you were meeting her there today, weren't you?"

"I was not!"

Dewey started singing, "Billie and Mabel Ann sitting in a tree..."

He'd gone too far. I walked up to him and shoved him down to the gravel road. He caught himself with his open palms, and I could tell by the way he looked at his hands while he sat on the ground that it stung. He popped up quickly and yelled, "I was just funning you, you bastard!"

"I didn't think it was that funny."

Dewey spit on each of his palms and rubbed them gently together. He looked up at me, and I must have had fire in my eyes because Dewey waved his hands at me and silently picked up his bike and rode away. As I saw him rolling down the road, he turned back once and flipped me off. I had never before given anyone the finger, but I made an exception that day for Dewey Barnes.

I turned back to look at the alien in the tree. As I had stared at it the first time, I had started putting together this whole scenario, about a group of aliens who had landed here centuries ago, before any white men had come to America, maybe even before any Indians lived here. They had landed in the forest here, made a camp, studied Earth nature, and then left. But before they left, they had imprinted their images psychically into all the trees around here. If you busted open any of these trees along this road, you might see this same image of these ancient astronauts.

As I looked at the tree now, all I saw was squiggly lines.

I pedaled back toward the Carasell place wondering if my imagination had concocted all the things that had happened to me there, just like I'd written a whole fantastic storyline in a matter of seconds when I stared at a tree struck by lightning. Perhaps Mabel Ann was a bad influence in all this, with her dead father and her anti-social behavior and the mysterious voices she heard in her head. Perhaps Mabel Ann really was crazy, and I was headed there myself.

I found myself back at the Carasell place, back where it all began, doubtful of myself and anything I experienced. My father didn't talk to me from the grave. I wasn't sliding back and forth in some crack in time. Everything that happened to me was completely explainable. Not that I had an explanation, but I didn't need one. I needed to accept things as they were. My father was dead, and whatever happened to him in the past was over, done with, and none of my business.

The sound that I heard next was loud and sharp, echoing all around me. So loud I hit the ground when I heard it, flying off my bike. I'd heard the sound before, but usually from far away, in the woods, or over a pond. This sound was right on top of me, like it came from just a few feet away. I looked up and surveyed the land around me. I saw no one anywhere. I was about to raise my head when I heard the sound again, almost identical, and I ducked. I lay there for several minutes, my hands over my head, waiting to hear the sound again, or worse, find out where it came from. Finally, I rose and looked. The world was peaceful. Crickets were chirping. No one was anywhere to be seen. But I was certain of one thing. I had heard gunshots. Two of them. Right there. And whether anyone else had heard them or not, they were real enough to me.

Chapter 13

I decided not to ride my bike to meet Lionel that afternoon. It was only a few blocks from my house to the corner where I'd met the factory worker the day before so there was really no reason to take it. And while I didn't want to believe what the nosey old lady at the window had told me, I just felt better knowing my bike was safe at home.

I made sure I got to the spot at least a few minutes before 3:00, so I wouldn't miss him. Rather than standing on the side of the road where the old lady lived, I found a spot on the opposite side of the intersection near a tree where I could stay out of her view. I didn't like the thought of her spying on me. She might actually call the cops if she saw me, and that would surely frighten off Lionel, which I didn't want to do.

I could tell it was after 3:00 when I saw a group of black men walking past the old lady's house and toward the railroad tracks. I watched carefully to see if the man I had met the day before was among them, but he wasn't. I also noticed a glare in the old lady's window and guessed it was her reflection as she took her daily post to watch for thieves. Why didn't she just move? Maybe she liked having someone to keep an eye on. Maybe it made her feel more alive. Maybe she liked the danger she perceived.

A couple of minutes passed, and I saw the man that I had seen from the day before, walking alone. I got a little rattled. He had promised to bring Lionel with him. Where was he? Even though I knew the old lady was studying the road, I took off from my spot behind the tree and raced up behind the man.

"Hey, mister! Stop."

The black man turned and saw me. "Well, you're here. Fancy that."

"Where's Lionel? You said you'd bring him with you."

"So I did." The man reached out his hand. "Mr. Williams. I'm Lionel Sumner. How are you?"

I shook Lionel's hand and sighed at how easily I'd been fooled by him. "Why didn't you tell me yesterday?" I asked.

"I was testing you. Wanted to see how serious you were."

I could feel the hairs on the back of my neck rising and turned to see the glare in the old lady's window. "Can we walk down the road a little ways. There's a lady over there that's watching us, and she makes me nervous."

"Oh, that's just Old Mrs. Wickham." Lionel announced as he turned and led me down the road. "She ain't no harm. Just a busybody. Got her lawnmower stolen a few years ago. Hadn't trusted anybody since then." Lionel stopped at the edge of the tracks and flopped down on the ground. "I sure am tired," he said. "Slapping the soles on them shoes all day will shore WEAR YOU OUT!"

He blew out a big rush of air, making a whistling sound with his lips. I stared at him. He looked up at me. "What is it you need, young Mr. Williams?"

"I want to know about something that happened to you, or may have happened to you, when you worked for my father."

"That was a long time ago. Lots happened since then. Lots been swept under the rug and forgotten."

"I'm just hoping you can answer some questions."

"Alright. Lay it on me."

"I've heard from a couple of people that you may have gotten in trouble with the law, and my daddy helped you."

"The Law," he said placing his left hand in front of him like he was about to shake hands, "...and me," he continued gesturing the same way with his right hand next to his left. "We tries to keep as much distance from each other as possible." He moved the two hands apart and smiled.

"But what about when you worked for my daddy?"

Lionel leaned back on his elbows. "Like I said, long time ago. Hard to remember."

"Are you saying that because it's hard to remember or because you don't want to talk about it?"

Lionel sat up quickly with a grim look and gave me a start. Almost as quickly, the serious expression melted into a smile. "You're a little too smart for your own good, son. Why do you want to know about all this that happened before you were even a twinkle in your mama's eye?"

"I have my reasons."

"Well, let's put it this way," Lionel said, rising off the ground. "I have my reasons, too. Good day, young Mr. Williams." Lionel turned and crossed the tracks.

I followed him up to the top of the hill where the tracks lay. "Did it have something to do with Harry Maxwell?" I shouted to him as he walked down the street.

He didn't turn back. Only raised up his hands as if to say, "I don't know." I watched him for several minutes as he faded in amongst the houses. I turned and looked down the tracks to see a black boy standing a hundred feet away from me, staring. I stared back at him for a few seconds, then walked back down the hill and toward my home. As I passed Mrs. Wickham's house, I crossed to the other side of the road and looked for just a second to see the glare in the window.

Chapter 14

If Lionel Sumner wouldn't talk to me, and Harry Maxwell was dead, and I had learned all there was to know from my mama and Don Butt and Sheriff Colby, I just didn't know where else to turn. Here's what I believed at this point: Something had happened at the house Harry Maxwell owned on Pickman Drive in the Macon neighborhood and my daddy was there when it happened. He told somebody to put something down, and there were shots that were fired—two of them. Lionel Sumner may or may not have been involved. He, for sure, had something to hide. Why any of this mattered now, twenty years later, I didn't know. Why I would get these wisps of information when I was near the location of that house was especially disturbing. I'd never had anything like that happen to me before so I had to believe there was something special about them. And they seemed so authentic. I didn't ask for any of this. I didn't want it. But I got it anyway.

I tried to return to my life. I tried to watch television, but John Dean was testifying every day on all three channels, and there was no escape. I tried to work on Mama's puzzle, but I just got distracted and bored. I even pulled out an old airplane model I never finished and tried to stick it together, but I kept slipping and breaking little pieces off of it. If Jim had been here, we could have played, and I could have gotten all this off my mind. But he wasn't and I was alone.

I was lying on my bed, staring at the light fixture on the ceiling and counting the cobwebs, when I heard a knock at the front door. I could have answered it myself, but I figured it was Miss Cynthia, our neighbor, coming to trade gossip with my mom. I heard Mama walk to the front door and the mumble of voices, and then she came to my door.

"You got a visitor."

I couldn't imagine who it was. I didn't want anything to do with Dewey Barnes and I'm sure he felt the same. Mark and Ronnie were busy trying to design some dangerous stunt and could care less about me. I came to the front door and walked onto the screened-in porch. Sitting in the porch swing was Mabel Ann, rocking back and forth and looking happy as a clam with a notebook sitting on her lap.

"Hey, Billy."

"What are you doing here?"

"Now, can't a person just come visit a friend without a reason?"

"Are we friends?"

"Don't be snotty, or I won't tell you what I found out."

I moved closer to her and spoke softly. "Found out about what?"

"About you know what."

I moved right up next to her. "So?"

"So, sit down and I'll tell you about it."

Oh boy, would Dewey Barnes have a field day with this! Me sitting in the front porch swing with Mabel Ann McCarthy.

"I went to see my friend, Mrs. Kelly, the librarian."

"You're friends with the librarian?"

"Why's that so odd? I like to read. She likes kids who read. Not much more to that story."

"Okay, so what did you ask her about?"

"The house at 453 Pickman Drive."

"Did she know something about it?"

"No, but she has a whole stack of newspapers and an index to them."

The Weir Chronicle had been in constant publication since 1893 when it was started by George Columbus. "The Who, What, When and Where of Weir" was the slogan at the top of the masthead. It was a weekly paper, and the Weir Public Library had a copy of every Weir Chronicle ever published except for a half dozen in 1943 when the Library moved to its current location. I had no idea there was an index.

"It's really not an index, it's a clip file. Mrs. Kelly started it herself several years ago. She would take the extra copies of the newspaper and clip out stories and put them in files for different categories."

"So there was a file on Harry Maxwell's house?"

"No, but there was a lot about it in a file called Crime."

I nodded my head and told her about my visit with Sheriff Colby. She opened up her notebook and ran her finger across some of the notes she'd jotted down. "Yeah, I found at least a half dozen times over the years that it was raided for gambling and moonshining. As late as 1968, some people were arrested there for drug possession."

"In 1968? Carasell must have owned it then."

"Yeah, I think he just kept up the bad reputation his uncle had started for the place." She reached back in the notebook and pulled out a piece of paper. "There was one story I got Mrs. Kelly to make a copy for me. It was from 1956. Take a look."

The headline read "Murder at Pickman Drive."

"Murder?"

"Yeah. Read it."

I read the story out loud. "The body of an unidentified man, who died of an apparent gunshot wound to the head, was found by authorities on Tuesday at the house at 453 Pickman Drive in Macon. The Weir Police Department currently has no suspects in the shooting. The house is a rental property owned by Harry Maxwell, who is currently residing in West Tennessee. The last tenants of the house are unknown. Police believe the man was shot three times to the head with a small caliber pistol." I looked at Mabel Ann. "Is that it?"

"Not exactly." She looked at her notebook. "The police eventually identified the man as 23-year-old Randy Wexman, who lived on Carter Street. As far as we could tell, they never caught the murderer."

"Did they talk to Maxwell?"

"It's not clear. There's only the story I gave you, a follow-up story about the identity of the body, and an editorial about the rising crime rate in Weir that mentions the murder. If the murder was solved, it didn't make it into Mrs. Kelly's files."

I sat there rocking quietly, trying to piece it together. "Put that down." "This is your LAST warning." Gunshots, but only two. Scenes from a murder. Is that what I'd been experiencing?

"I wonder why Sheriff Colby didn't tell me about this."

"Maybe he didn't remember it. You said he was pretty sick."

"He seemed to remember everything else about Harry Maxwell."

"Maybe this didn't involve Harry Maxwell. Just because it happened at his house didn't mean he was involved in it. Besides this was the Weir Police Department investigating, not the sheriff's office."

"So do you think my father could have been there, the night this murder took place?"

"There's an even bigger question, Billy."

I looked at her. Her face was set like stone.

"Do you think your father could have been the one who pulled the trigger?"

That was not a question I wanted to think about at this point. I stood up and marched to the other end of the porch and paced, looking down.

"I mean, it's not like it's cold-blooded murder. He might have been trying to protect himself."

I looked up. "Might have been? What else could it be, but self-protection? Did they find any other weapons there?"

"It doesn't say anything about it in the first story, and there's nothing about it later. I'd think if the police had found a weapon in the house, it would have made it into the newspaper."

"Not much made it into the newspaper at all. I'm surprised they ever printed the guy's name. What was it again?"

"Randy Wexman. I asked Mrs. Kelly if she'd ever heard the name, and she couldn't recall."

"What did you tell Mrs. Kelly about why you were looking this stuff up?"

"I just told her I'd seen where the house had burned down and wondered if there was anything in the newspapers about the house."

"Did you mention my name?"

"No, of course not."

"Did you tell her that you thought your friend's father had killed this man?"

"No, I didn't. Stop looking at me like that."

I realized just how confused and paranoid this story had made me. I wanted to blame someone for what we discovered and Mabel Ann was right there. I must have looked at her with a lot of rage.

I turned away and walked off the front porch. Mabel Ann followed me. "I'm sorry, Billy. I thought you'd want to know."

"I did. But now I'm not so sure." I picked up my bike from the front yard and sailed away, leaving Mabel Ann standing in my front yard, her notebook clasped tightly to her chest. I thought I heard her sniffle as I rode out of sight.

Chapter 15

I was headed back to the Carasell house, the Maxwell place, 453 Pickman Drive, the concrete slab. So many names, so little truth. I so desperately wanted to know what happened that night in 1956, but at the same time, I didn't want to know. The truth is very smelly, sometimes, like rotten meat or spoiled eggs, garbage dumps or burned-up houses. Nothing sweet to it at all.

I arrived at the concrete slab and took my place in the middle of it, concentrating, waiting for a sign, a sound. I sat there, listening intently, waiting for instruction, hoping for an explanation. All I heard was crickets and the distant sound of someone hammering. The magic was gone.

I must have sat there for a couple of hours before I gave up. The sun was starting to droop toward the horizon, and it was getting late. The skeeters had come out and I was getting eaten alive. I was headed back to my bike when I heard the roar of Justin Carasell's Gran Torino. The car stopped on the road in front of me, and Carasell shouted out of his window.

"Kid, are you still hanging around here?"

"Yeah. How about you? You get your money yet?"

"Not yet, but I'm close. The investigators decided it was a leaky gas pipe that caused the fire. The police are satisfied, but the insurance company is still balking. That's how insurance is."

I walked up to his window. "Did you know there was murder here back in the 50s?"

"A murder!" Carasell's eyes shifted to the left. "Y'know, I think my uncle told me something about that. Some fellow got himself shot, didn't he?"

"Yeah."

"Too bad the place burned down. Where's a ghost gonna live if his haunted house is destroyed?"

"What do you mean by that?"

"Nothing. Just seems like you always hear about ghosts where a murder's taken place."

"If you get your money, are you gonna build a new place here?"

"Hell no. I'm going to sell this land and use the money to move to California."

"California? What's out there?"

"Beautiful women, sunny beaches, movie stars. The life, man."

"I hear there's lots of smog and crime and earthquakes."

"Hey, everything's got its ups and downs, kid. You got to hang in there and enjoy the best part." Carasell pulled out a cigarette. "Hey, your folks wouldn't be interested in this prime piece of real estate, would they? You hang around here so much, you must like it."

"No, I don't like it at all. And my mama doesn't have any money to spend."

"Too bad. I think you could build a nice little cottage right there. Good place to live. Except for the ghosts, that is. See ya, kid!" Carasell put his foot to the floor, and the Torino squealed as he roared away.

I rode back to my house, and Mama scolded me for being out so late. It was nearly dark when I came through the door, and while Mama didn't mind me riding all over town during the day, she didn't like me staying out past sundown. "Bad things happen after dark," she said.

I picked at my supper that night. Too bad because it was pork chops and fried potatoes. Good stuff, but the day's revelations had stolen my appetite. Mama thought I was sick and sent me on to bed. It was just as well. I had that feeling you get when nothing's going right, and all you want to do is sleep. But when you sleep, it's not a tired sleep, like you been working all day and deserve the rest. It's a restless, tossing-and-turning sleep, which is exactly what I had that night. I kept seeing images of my father standing there in Harry Maxwell's house, pointing a gun at some young guy and shooting his head off. In all the years since my dad had died, I'd never had a bad thought about him. He was a hero in our family, a man who stood up for what was right and took care of those that were in trouble. He was a good man, an honest man, the kind of man you could count on. But I'd only known him for four years and those memories were vague and uncertain. Most of what I knew about my father I had learned from other people – stories that my mother told and my sisters. Stories from Don Butt and from my brother who lived in Arizona and only showed up about once every two or three years. No one speaks ill of the dead, so maybe all those stories were just a smoke screen. Maybe my dad was not the saint I'd always heard about. Maybe this was the message that I was being delivered from beyond. Get real! Your dad's just like the rest of the human population. His feet are made of clay. Not granite. Certainly not gold.

I slept late the next day. Mama checked on me a couple of times. Came into my room and placed the back of her hand on my forehead. We never owned a thermometer. Mama could tell if you had a temperature just from her gentle touch. I guess I was okay because she didn't make me take any pills.

When I finally did get up, it was lunchtime, and she'd made tomato soup, always the best thing for someone under the weather, even if he wasn't running a fever. I smashed up some saltines and turned the soup into a kind of a mush. It tasted good, especially since I'd missed two meals already. After lunch, Mama let me watch TV, even though it was time for her soap operas. The Watergate hearings were on recess today, so everything was back to normal.

When I saw the clock strike 3:00, I thought about the day shift at the shoe factory getting off work. Some of them would be getting in their cars and rushing away, and some would be walking. That group of black men would be laughing and kidding with each other as they walked past old Mrs. Wickham's house. And Mrs. Wickham would be staring at them through the window and fretting about which of them was going to steal her potted plants or her hedge clippers or the angel from her birdbath in the backyard. And then there'd be Lionel Sumner, walking alone, whistling to himself, secrets tied up tight inside his chest he didn't want to share with anyone.

I leapt off the couch and headed out the door. Mama yelled after me, "Where are you going? Aren't you sick?"

"I'm feeling fine now. I'll be back in a little bit."

I grabbed my bike and raced down the road to the place where I knew Lionel Sumner would be crossing the tracks. It was already a few minutes past 3, so I rushed on past Mrs. Wickham's house to the hill where the tracks sat and looked over into the neighborhood on the other side. About three blocks away, I saw Lionel walking with his back to me. I gritted my teeth and for the first time in my life I rolled down the hill and onto the west side of the tracks, where all the black folks in Weir lived. I rode up to Lionel, just as he neared the front door of a little green house with an unpainted fence.

"Mr. Sumner!"

Lionel turned and seemed shocked to see a little white boy standing on his bike in his front yard. The front door of his house opened, and a boy stood there, staring at me. I guessed it was Lionel Sumner, Jr.

"What are you doing here?"

"I know you don't want to talk to me, and I know there's something happened to you that you don't want anybody to know about, but I've got to have some answers, and you're probably the only person in the world that can tell me the truth."

Lionel stared at me for a full minute before he said a thing. He turned toward the door and told his son, "Get on in the house. I'll be there d'rectly." The boy walked inside and shut the door. Lionel sat down on his porch steps and pulled out a pipe.

"You're a persistent cuss."

"Yes sir."

Lionel took a match from his pocket and began puffing on his pipe lighting it. Once the pipe was lit, he padded the space next to him, inviting me to sit there.

"If I tell you what happened, what are you gonna do about it?"

"Nothing."

"You ain't gonna go blabbing to the police or telling the news-papers or nothing, are you?"

"No sir."

"Expect there ain't many folk left who care one way or another anyway. Except you."

Chapter 16

On that afternoon, so many years ago, Lionel Sumner told me what happened.

When Mr. Sumner was 17, he worked for my Daddy as a field hand. He always hired four or five black men to work for him during harvest time. I guess he would have hired white men if he'd wanted to, but blacks worked for minimal wages, and Daddy didn't have much money to spend. Mr. Sumner had worked for him two seasons in a row, and Daddy had grown to like him. Mr. Sumner told me he was a hard worker and always had a good story to tell, something Daddy valued.

In the fall of 1956, after the crops were harvested, Mr. Sumner had fallen into a rough crowd. He'd taken the money that he'd earned working on Daddy's farm and spent it on Harry Maxwell's floating crap game. He had a winning streak for a while, and Harry didn't like that so he made sure Mr. Sumner started losing. And losing big.

When Mr. Sumner came to Harry Maxwell and told him he was all out of money, and that his mama would kick him out of the house if he didn't pay his way, Mr. Maxwell offered him some work, collecting debts on the black side of town.

"I wasn't hardly big enough or mean enough to be very good as a skull-cracker," Mr. Sumner told me, "but I was a pretty good actor. So I used to walk into somebody's house and shout and scream and threaten their children and it wasn't long before they were rummaging through their sock drawers for all the extra money they'd hidden away for emergencies."

Mr. Sumner was doing a good job making collections for Mr. Maxwell, so he decided to give him some extra work. He had him make calls on the white side of the tracks. Generally, Mr. Maxwell would hire a black man to work the black gamblers, and a white man to work the white gamblers, but the white man he'd hired had turned out to be a lazy drunkard so Mr. Maxwell thought he'd try Lionel out on the eastern side of the tracks.

"I didn't like that idea one bit. It was one thing if a Negro got caught shaking down folks on his side of town, but if I was to be caught threatening a white man, I might just get invited to a necktie party, if you know what I mean."

Mr. Maxwell was insistent and threatened to turn Mr. Sumner over to the police. He bragged that all the policemen in town were in his pocket and would do whatever he said. Mr. Sumner got scared and ran. He ran all the way to Daddy's farm.

"I told your Daddy every stitch of the truth. He didn't scold me or shame me or nothin'. Just nodded his head and said he understood. Said everybody had their bad days when they were young and none of us should be held to account for the mistakes we made when we were kids."

Mr. Sumner told my Daddy that Maxwell was looking for him and that he might be sending the cops after him. Daddy decided he could hide him at an old pump house on the backside of his property. Daddy often took his meals with him into the field, so he could feed him without even telling his wife about it. He could hole up there for a while, and when the heat had calmed down, move on. The pump house was situated in such a way that it had a clear view of the farmhouse so Lionel would just have to keep his eyes peeled and if he saw anyone headed his way, he could just take off into the woods that were right behind him.

A couple of weeks passed and the only lawman who came to my Daddy's place was Sheriff Colby. "I saw him when he drove up in his old brown sedan with the blue lights, and I was ready to sprint into the woods if I needed to, but your Daddy told him that he hadn't seen me since harvesting time and suggested the Sheriff spend his time doing something more useful."

Daddy had told Mr. Sumner that the Sheriff didn't seem much interested in finding him anyway. It was really more the city police's concern, but he was just doing them a favor. Daddy suggested that Harry Maxwell might be behind the whole thing, and the Sheriff hated Maxwell. He told Daddy not to worry about it, that he'd see to it that the police backed off. Mr. Sumner couldn't quite explain it, but there was some gentleman's agreement between the city police and the Sheriff about what they would and wouldn't do, and this crossed the line.

After a week, my Daddy called the Sheriff and asked him whether the police were still looking for Mr. Sumner, and the Sheriff said the warrant against him had been lifted for lack of evidence. Daddy gave Mr. Sumner the good news and told him he ought to move on to some other town and not go back to Weir.

"I agreed it was a good idea, but I had to say goodbye to my mama before I left. She didn't know what happened to me, and she'd be worried sick if she didn't see me again."

When he came back to his mama's house, the house we were sitting in front of as he told me the story, a big white guy was waiting for him. Mr. Maxwell had hired a new skull-cracker in the time since Lionel had left. The white guy threw Mr. Sumner in the trunk of his car and drove him to Maxwell's "rental house" on Pickman Drive in Macon.

"As that son-of-a-bitch was stuffing me in the back of his car, I yelled to my mama, 'Call Mr. Williams! Call Mr. Williams!' I knew the police wouldn't care, but Mr. Williams would."

Mr. Sumner's mother called my Daddy and through the crying and blubbering told him what had happened. Daddy felt enormous guilt for letting Mr. Sumner go back to his mother's house. He should have insisted that he leave town. He had no idea where Maxwell's thug would have taken Lionel, so he called the Sheriff and told him about the distressed call he'd gotten from his mother. The Sheriff told him he'd have to stay out of it. It was all part of that gentlemen's agreement between him and the city police, but he told my Daddy that the thug had most likely taken Lionel to the house on Pickman Drive.

"When your Daddy got there, that white boy had me all tied up with electrical tape. I think he was gonna burn me alive because he had a gallon of gasoline sitting on the table and a box of matches. Your daddy started pounding on the front door, and the white boy just turned off the lights and sat there quietly, pointing his gun at me and warning me to stay still."

Daddy walked to the back of the house and could see Mr. Sumner through the kitchen window. He'd carried a crowbar with him from his truck and used it to smash in the back door. The thug had his back against the wall as Daddy came through and turned to point his gun at him. Daddy shouted, "Put that down! Put that down now!" The thug did not comply.

"Listen, mister, I'm gonna give you a chance to get out of here. You just turn around and go back where you came and pretend like none of this ever happened."

Daddy just stood there, staring at him.

"You're a white man. Are you really willing to give your life for this boy?"

"Sometimes, you just got to stand up, even when you feel like falling down."

The thug didn't understand what he meant. "This is your LAST warning! Get out of here, or I'm gonna shoot you and pile your body on top of his and let the coroner sort out the bits and pieces."

"Well, if you're gonna shoot me, go ahead and shoot me. Let's see what you're made of."

"The next thing I heard," explained Mr. Sumner, "was two gunshots. It was dark but I was pretty sure that white boy had shot and killed your Daddy. I cried. There was never a man so good to me. Then all of a sudden, I saw that white boy sliding down the wall. I heard voices and outside the door. I saw Sheriff Colby. I guess he'd snuck up behind your daddy and got a bead on that boy and shot him before he could even press the trigger."

Despite the gentlemen's agreement, Sheriff Colby had followed Daddy to the house on Pickman Drive and when it looked like he might be shot, drew his revolver and took down the thug—one Randy Wexman of Carter Street. As they stripped the electrical tape off of Mr. Sumner, the Sheriff explained they'd have to cover this up. If it was discovered that the Sheriff had shot one of Maxwell's men, it would cause a big stink. The Sheriff explained that the law in a small town like Weir was a complicated machine, and if anyone knocked the gears out of place, it was hell trying to get it to run right again. They were packing up the gasoline and the electrical tape for Papa to carry off in his pickup when Wexman made a grunting sound. The Sheriff pulled out his gun and plugged him again, this time for the last time.

"Your father carried me that night to Forrest City and told me to stay there until things blew over. It wasn't until about five years ago that I moved back here to Weir, after my mama passed. I was shore sad to hear that your Daddy had passed while I was gone, too. He was a good man. Risked his life for me. I still don't really know why."

That afternoon, I told Mr. Sumner how I'd talked with Sheriff Colby a few days ago and that he'd mentioned his name but didn't seem to remember him.

"I guess I'm not surprised about that. He's getting pretty old. I probably wasn't the only colored boy that got in some trouble with Harry Maxwell."

"Yeah, but I bet you were the only one the Sheriff shot someone to save and then had to cover up."

"Don't be kidding yourself, boy. The Sheriff didn't shoot that white boy to save me. He did it to save your Daddy. If your Daddy hadn't come along, that house on Pickman Drive would've burned down 17 years ago, and not a couple of months ago. And with me in it."

Chapter 17

After lisening to Mr. Sumner, I slowly rode back to my house. I felt like a great weight had been lifted from me. Just knowing what had happened was such a relief. I wondered if I should tell Mama the story of Lionel Sumner and Sheriff Colby and the house on Pickman Drive. Maybe she knew all about it and just had sworn never to tell anyone, like I had.

I decided not to tell her. This story was between me and Daddy. I'm sure she had plenty of stories she hadn't told me about. This was the only one I had that belonged strictly to me. There was one person, however, that deserved to hear the whole thing. Mabel Ann. As weird a character as she was, she'd been a good friend to me. Sticking by me, even when I sounded stupid, and even sticking her neck out to find some clues herself. But she was such a mess! How would I ever be friends with her without making myself look bad.

I went to bed peacefully that night, falling to sleep with the glow of the streetlight on the miniature Ford Galaxie. I dreamed that night of my father and the Galaxie. He was driving me through town. Down Front Street by Meyer's Grocery. Over on Elm Street, where Aunt Velma lived. Down Billings to Maple and past Mabel Ann's house and on up to Saratoga Hills, where I sneered at Dewey Barnes. Then over to Macon and down Pickman Drive. We stopped in front of Mr. Maxwell's house. It wasn't burned down.

It was standing there, a little white frame house with a rusty old car sitting out front. Daddy proceeded to tell me all about what happened to him there in that house. About his telling Wexman "to put that gun down," and Wexman telling him it was "his last warning," and about the gun shots. He only mentioned two.

When I stirred, I had the strangest thought. Maybe Daddy really had driven me by the house on Pickman. Maybe he had told me all those things when I was two or three years old, like it was some kind of modern fairytale. Maybe it sat on the edge of my memory, like those other things I remembered about him—the secret trip to see Santa Claus and letting me drive the car while I sat in his lap and getting lost in the rice field. Maybe it was just waiting to be unleashed and when I saw the Carasell house all burned out, it all came back to me in a flash. Is that possible?

Good grief, it made more sense than ghosts haunting me or time travel or that I was just going bonkers.

I rode over to Mabel Ann's house first thing the next day. She was playing in the front yard with Groucho, just like I'd seen her on the first time. I told her I had quite a tale to tell her and that she should leave Groucho behind. Instead of going to the Carasell place, I rode her on the back of my bike to the little city park downtown. I'd saved up a little money, so I bought her an ice cream cone from the drug store and we sat under the maple trees, and I told her the whole story. I even told her about the dream I had and that I thought maybe my daddy had told me the whole story, and I was just remembering it in dribs and drabs. She crunched a bite of her cone and looked me straight in the eye and said, "Yeah, but wouldn't it be a lot more fun to think you were getting messages from another dimension?"

I thought about it for a moment and had to agree. I wondered just how much of Mabel Ann's "voices" and "visions" were just "more fun" than what they really were—her acting out. She was a smart girl and brave, but she really didn't fit anywhere. Neither did I for that matter, but I was quiet enough and passive enough to seem to fit. Mabel Ann just didn't care about fitting. She liked who she was even if everybody else thought she was a nutjob.

I heard a shout from down the road. It was Dewey Barnes. He was riding with Mark Twilley, Ronnie Rodgers and Laura Kindren.

"Spooning with your girlfriend, Billy?" Dewey asked in the most mocking tone possible.

I stood up on the seat of the picnic table. "She's not my girlfriend!" I shouted. I looked over at Mabel Ann, who seemed like she was about to pout. "But she is my friend friend." Her expression changed immediately, and she looked proud and confident, as she finished off the last bite of her ice cream cone.

There was a silence among us, for what seemed like hours. In actuality, it was probably only thirty seconds.

Ronnie spoke first. "We were going down to that ditch on the other side of town. Mark says it's a good place for riding motocross." Ronnie looked around at the others, then back at me. "You wanta come with us?"

I stared into Dewey's eyes, which stared hard back at me. Then his gaze broke, and he rolled his eyes up. "Ah, c'mon," he said in surrender, and turned his bike away from us.

I turned to Mabel Ann. "Do you want to go?"

"But I can't ride," she said.

Mark spoke up, "Then it's about time someone taught you how."

Epilogue

The Watergate hearings continued on television until August 7, 1973. It was said about 85 percent of American households tuned in for at least part of the coverage. They were probably just hoping to see their favorite TV show. While the hearings were over, the investigation stretched on for another year. On August 8, 1974, President Richard Nixon addressed the nation and told them he would resign at noon the next day, and Gerald Ford would be sworn in as president. Nixon had made mistakes, that was certain, but he'd also done some good things in office, like opening up peace talks with the Soviets and the Chinese. He started the Environmental Protection Agency and signed the Clean Air Act. He made the first long distance call to the moon when he spoke to the Apollo 11 crew, and he approved funding for the Space Shuttle program.

And his blunder, Watergate, led a young boy in a small town in Arkansas to go ride his bike and discover something about his father he never would have known.

www.ingramcontent.com/pod-product-compliance
Lightning Source LLC
Chambersburg PA
CBHW020625250626
47154CB00004B/1669